BROKEN MIRRORS
NARCISSISM and NARCISSISTS,
SHORT STORIES and METAPHORS

I0531103

John Smale

Author of

SPOTTING, COPING, ESCAPING AND
RECOVERING FROM NARCISSISTS;
Love Bombing and Coercive Control

www.emp3books.com

Published in September 2022 by emp3books Ltd
6 Silvester Way, Church Crookham, GU52 0TD

©John Smale 2022

ISBN: 9781910734513

www.emp3books.com

CONTENTS

OTHER BOOKS
by John Smale

*****

SPOTTING, COPING, ESCAPING AND RECOVERING FROM NARCISSISTS; Love Bombing and Coercive Control

*****

STOP BELIEVING THE LIES, BELIEVE IN YOURSELF

*****

MIND CHANGING SHORT STORIES AND METAPHORS; for Hypnosis, Hypnotherapy & NLP

*****

MOVING FORWARD; life changing short stories and metaphors

*****

SHORT STORIES AND METAPHORS, beneficial short stories and metaphors

*****

HYPNOTHERAPY, the essentials of treatment: causes, effects and strategies for effective treatment with hypnosis, hypnotherapy and NLP

INTRODUCTION

Having written and published, **Spotting, Coping, Escaping and Recovering from Narcissists,** two things became apparent.

There is a huge demand for help with tackling narcissism and this book has been published as an aid for that.

The other thing is that the readers want to read and/or listen in private, away from prying eyes. It became like my sessions when I listened to my clients and discovered ways to help them. We worked with stories and metaphors that related to their problems and helped them to find relief, and gave them the determination to escape from them. It was always completely private.

In the past I have shared those stories in widely read books with, of course, no references to the people I helped, and a lot of those were about narcissistic abuse. A very small number of those are included towards the end of this book as bonus reading.

My aim with this publication is a simple one. To help the sufferers of the huge number of emotional predators. Those people actually feed on the victim's desire to help and cure them. That is difficult to the point of impossibility because narcissism is a psychological disorder and no amount of attention can help them to get better, but the effort put in is what the controllers demand and devour.

So, this is the emergency exit, the way out, for readers or their friends who are in the position of being trapped in an unhappy and destructive relationship that will end in tears unless something positive is done.

A note about spelling. This book, although containing some stories about American people, uses UK English. My apologies if some of the spellings look strange.

OPEN PRISON WALLS

Sometimes we are not kept in solid walls but in an emotional trap such as fear in an abusive relationship. The following poem refers to that.

I feel so hemmed in by prison walls
That do not exist. So why not escape?
If there are no walls the route
To freedom is an easy path.

And because the bonds that tie and trap me
Cannot be felt or seen, I cannot break them.
I'm unable to push through walls that
Are not there, and so I can't escape.

But because they don't exist I can't describe them,
Yet they still contain me.
Yet, if I walk forwards then
I can walk through them.

Those walls that only exist in my mind
Are made from nothing that can keep me
From enjoying what should be enjoyed.
They cannot keep me in.

Prison walls are made from fears of losing the false desire. The hope of a better life is the real dream and it is what helps us to see reality and enables us to escape from what is trapping us because our emotions are feeding others.

The other stories will show where the real emergency exits are.

BROKEN MIRRORS

George had a favourite mirror. It was big, well lit and reflected his perfect face and body. He found it sexy and when he stared into it, the mirror told the truth about how wonderful he was.

When he was young, his mother worried about his obsession with gazing into mirrors. 'Just look at yourself.' She would say, and that is what he did, and kept on doing for the rest of his life.

Now he was older, he added the joys of selfies to mirror images. These images were so very different.

He could make montages for display on social media because the whole world needed to see what a handsome catch he was for any lucky woman who wanted to adore him. The main issue he had was getting a picture that showed him in all his glory; his good looks, the attractiveness of a film star and the charisma that he possessed. He was good at editing his selfies, with the help of green screens and photoshop, he could be on a tropical beach, at the peak of a mountain, surfing big waves, being surrounded by beautiful women. These filled his empty life but made onlookers envious. Perhaps they would become attracted to such a successful man who obviously achieved his goals.

Whereas the camera was a good friend, his mirror was not. It did not reflect the real image that he liked so much. Therefore, to correct what he saw to what other people saw, he bought another one so that he could see the mirror image of his mirror image which was how his magnificence was seen by others.

Yet, that was still not enough. His mirrors and selfies never spoke to him, never told him how wonderful he was. He thought he was clever and he told the mirror everything that he wanted to be told by admirers. He explained that he was in need of such a huge amount of praise because life had been tough. He had been orphaned when young. No, he had been abused. No, he had been hurt emotionally by people who had doubted his trust.

Yes, that was good because he had been untrustworthy, had cheated, had hurt others but nobody needed to know the truth.

He imagined the mirror talking to him with sympathy and a need to help him to overcome all of the wrong that had been done to him. He became bored with the lack of response and told his mirror that he would find others to look into to get a better response.

The travelling fair was coming to town and he decided to visit it in search of a diversion of his thoughts.

The fast and furious rides were too much for him but as he was so macho, he refused to go on the more gentle ones. He wandered around and then he saw his dream, a hall of mirrors, where he could see himself in all sorts of ways that he could admire.

He bought his ticket, walked in and gasped. There were so many of him, it was a paradise full of Georges.

One made him look tall, another short. He swore at the second but praised the first. In a similar way he appraised the images from fat to thin, rippled to smooth. He loved it.

They were like the women in his life. If they were unable to reflect back the image he wanted, the appreciation he craved, the sense of reliance that he wanted them to have; then he could just walk away and find the next one that was better at telling him the truth about how fantastic he was.

He made notes in his head about which mirrors he would buy to create his own amusement park at home.

He had everything set up after a few weeks. He let the mirrors see the competition, he could parade around in his smart clothes or naked so that he could be revered and respected by his harem of glass.

Women were good targets but they could be fickle and complain about his need for control and the demands he made that they suppress their own feelings so that they could just concentrate on making him happy.

He got the real thing from his mirrors that were able to show him what he yearned for, a reflection of how he really was. He was aware that he was such a perfect catch, he could use women as the mirrors. He would place one in his life and then add others to use when he needed to have his fix of attention and esteem. He had done that so many times before but his love of his own image was the real love of his life. He had so much in common with what he saw.

As a thought, he decided to name each mirror after the women he knew and had known. He could display himself and criticise each and every ex by name and tell them exactly how stupid they were not to do more to make the relationship work. He knew he put everything he had into charming them and it was their own fault if he got upset and angry. They were always to blame for him walking away for days at a time, cutting off contact. He was patient enough to wait for them to miss him and then beg for his return. If they did not, well, he knew it was because they were not good enough for him and were doing him a big favour.

Those who wanted him back needed to be shown how mad they were and he would correct their thinking when they thought differently to the way things actually were.

One day, fate kicked in with a mighty bang. The jet plane flew over his house and although forbidden, made a sonic boom that hurt his ears. He watched as each mirror cracked and started to fall to the floor. Each shard of glass made a clattering sound as it broke and shattered. Splinters bounced and cut his face badly. He would be scarred for evermore. He would never be as beautiful as he had been.

Picking up a large piece of the broken mirror, he looked at his new image and punished the reflection by throwing it against the

7

wall where it smashed even more, throwing out splinters that cut him even more.

That should be end of the story but George, being a narcissist, decided that his new rugged look would give him the chance to get sympathy from girls and women. It opened a new door for him. He would, from now on, use the soft and vulnerable flesh of a human admirer as his looking glass. They would be more trusting of him.

However, his plan never worked. A man with a scarred face is one thing, but a man with a shattered egotistical mind is something very different.

TWO'S COMPANY

That expression applies to relationships but there is something that Joan had not considered, getting pregnant with Wayne. The three of them would be a happy family and perhaps there would be more children to bond them all together in blissful parenthood. For him, two was company but three would be a crowd.

For Wayne, there was a balance to be made. He knew that he would have less attention than he had before and certainly less than he wanted.

He was unable to understand why Joan was so happy. To him, this was just another child being deposited into the world that would put pressure on their relationship. He had no feelings of joy at becoming a father. Instead he complained that there would be an extra mouth to feed.

The positive side of the situation was that Joan would be tied to the house looking after the baby and that would prevent her from going out and perhaps meeting other people. He also knew that a woman with a new child was less of an attractive proposition to another man. He knew that in nature, lions would kill the offspring of a rival in order to make more room for his, but that would not happen. Nobody would want a woman who had given birth to another's child.

Plus things were looking brighter as the new arrival would become a negotiating tool for more attention. He could threaten to leave Joan and the child unsupported and desperate for money unless she gave him more and more of what he lived for, admiration, praise and her sacrifice.

It was a win/win situation for the most part, the downside being having something that would have to compete for her displays of love and the child would need attention for feeds and changing.

There again, while Joan was busy then he could go out to find more supply of his needs from other women. Then, if he got caught out, he had his get-out-of-jail-free card to play, the son they would soon have. Wayne wanted to know what gender the child would be for reasons he did not know at that point.

As Joan's body shape changed, Wayne put her down. He talked about stretch marks; how her breasts were getting too big and saggier; how her face was getting rounder and anything else he could pick on that put her down. Most men have a growing love for a soon to be mother and saw her as more beautiful with every passing day. For a man who only thinks about himself and who demands his women to look as he wanted them to, this was all too much.

When Lucas was born, Wayne was away and his first questions were not about Joan or the baby but they concerned the look of the doctor involved, his age and his manner. He hated the idea that some other man had seen Joan naked.

Once he had heard the answers that concealed the details of the young and dashing doctor told differently as an old and wrinkled man, Wayne was satisfied enough to return to the woman he had been seeing in a town miles away while Joan was confined, and to be fed with sweet words about what a great father he would be.

When Joan and Lucas arrived back home, the young child was presented to 'daddy' for inspection. He was studied as closely as a forensics expert would have done. Wayne was looking for proof that the boy was his and not from a fling Joan might have had with a secret lover.

He was vaguely satisfied that the blanket wrapped infant might be his, but he would never be totally sure.

The real problems came to light when Joan pulled back her gown and presented a breast to the child.

They were Wayne's breasts and they were not to be shared, especially with a male.

He shouted at Joan and told her that she would have to use formula milk instead. He made up all sorts of nonsense about how bad human milk was and how the best start in life came from something that had been specifically made for humans.

He got angry when she told him that breast milk was exactly that. Something produced to succour and nurture human babies. After slapping her face, Wayne stormed out after repeating that it was forbidden.

It all got worse and worse as Joan's attention was taken by her son and, rather than figuring out that mothers have love for both their partners and their children, his lack of understanding meant that he could not share in the joy of being a father.

The threats of violence became acts of physical hurt. He would punch her where the marks would not show to anybody apart from her secret lover that he assumed she had and who was probably the father of this handicap in his life.

Wayne paid no attention to his son. He was just a 'thing' that took away his feed of consideration and care from Joan. He was a parasite of the relationship that Wayne had worked so hard at to achieve. He had a reliant woman in his life who he moulded to fit his needs like a tailor who makes the perfect fitting suit. He needed more than Joan was able to give him. There was another person in her and his life.

He, as would be expected, sought his supplies of the love drug elsewhere. He needed his fixes on a continual basis and if he could not get total devotion from Joan, it was only right that she suffered a torrent of abuse and a stream of accusations while he gathered what he needed from whoever he could persuade and charm into giving it.

Joan was lonely. She wanted to show off her son to her parents, her siblings, her friends and the whole world, but her contacts with those others had been shrunk to the point where Joan could not risk upsetting Wayne by doing things behind his back.

Two years later, nothing positive had happened. Wayne believed that Lucas was still sucking the complimentary words and acts out of Joan, who had to go along with the flow to prevent her young infant from being physically hurt. The threats were made and she needed to protect herself and her child from being beaten with fists or insults.

The ring on the doorbell took Joan by surprise. Wayne had not been around for a while and she wondered if the caller was him. She opened the door, Lucas was standing next to her and smiled at the woman.

This stranger confirmed that it was Joan and that the young lad was Lucas before handing over a piece of paper. Joan read the law firm's name and the contents that said that Wayne was claiming custody of his son.

The woman tried to grab Lucas's hand and Joan punched her. Then she slammed the door and burst into tears.

A little while later, the police arrived and demanded that Lucas be handed over to his father on the grounds that Joan was a bad mother and violent. The punch that the woman had received was mentioned as further proof.

Unfortunately, Joan had no witnesses to the love and care she gave Lucas and would not be able to build a case based on the truth. Wayne held the trump cards and would ensure that he had enough proof against Joan, all of which would be made up but verified by his cronies.

This was never going to be custody for Lucas's protection or for a father's affection. It was all about punishing Joan for being a loving mother.

When the day in court arrived, Joan went along with a young

and cheap lawyer who would do his best against Wayne's top notch specialist in custody cases. That was all she could afford and she had to borrow money to pay him. All went well for Wayne until, near the end of the case, a woman walked into the courtroom, demanded to be heard as a witness on behalf of Joan and was invited to the dock.

She announced herself as Sheila, the head of a refuge for battered women and was involved with welfare for victims of domestic abuse. She told the court about three women who had all been victimised, debased and physically hurt by Wayne during the previous few years. She handed the judge statements signed by the victims and certified by a lawyer.

Wayne started shouting. He called this woman all the foul names that cannot be repeated and finished off by saying she was biased because he knew her and she wanted revenge. This was another lie. 'And anyway, that bitch, those bitches deserved what they got for cheating on me.' He knew he had put his foot into his own mouth.

Then the next testament by Sheila was the clincher. She explained that Wayne had been investigated by a private detective on behalf of the women he had hurt after his name kept on being mentioned. The proofs of his physical and emotional violence were well documented.

After being reported as a bad mother by Wayne to the social services to build his case, Joan had been watched and checked to find if she was at fault in the relationship with Wayne. She came out with a glowing report as being the perfect mother.

On his way out of court, an angry and spiteful man, his arm was grabbed by a policeman and he was charged with the assault of three women.

Joan never knew why she felt sorry for Wayne until it was explained that she was missing the well disguised charmer she had first met and that seemed to have clouded her view of what a monster he was in reality. It was all an illusion, she knew. The handsome prince had turned into an ugly frog.

It took her a while to erase all links with him and to recover the woman she had been before being caught, imprisoned and brain-washed into being his servant who provided what he demanded.

She parented Lucas on her own until one day she met a man at the playgroup. His daughter went there as well. Their relationship grew at a normal pace rather than the lightning romance she had with Wayne as he love bombed her. After a few years those close friends became the ideal partners for each other.

OLIVIA AND OLIVER

Walking a mile in somebody else's shoes is either a revelation or a catastrophe.

When a person's name is so similar to a famous character in literature, then fun for others is not far away especially as the woman was so self-centred.

She was known as 'More' following Oliver's request in the Charles Dickens story. Not that Olivia wanted more gruel, she wanted more from life and she wanted it now.

One man was not enough. She wanted more than just her devotee, she needed a few of them. She a fussy person in the cocktail bar where she was. Positioned on a stool that allowed her to look at her reflection in the mirror, she flicked her auburn hair and settled down.

She knew that if she sipped on a Bloody Mary and it would warm her, then she would need a Pina Colada to cool her down. Maybe that helped for a while but when its effect wore off, when it stopped pleasing her, then she looked at the list of mixtures to see what else was available.

She found that tiresome and asked the barman what would satisfy her, make her feel warm inside and for her to want more.

Leo, the barman was off her wish list, beneath her standards, but he was a good person to practice her 'come-on' looks with, as she looked around for the most attractive and prosperous man she could spot.

Being her, it was not in her repertoire to make a move on the guy she had chosen who was sitting at a table with a glass of wine and a book. She was the prize and he had to play hard to get it.

She already had her prize, herself. She had stolen the boyfriends of her two best friends, and had dumped them quickly. They were not what she wanted, her goal was to stop others from having a relationship that threatened her hold on them. She had explained that if their men had cheated, then they were better off without them. Strangely to others, they bought her story.

The man picked up his phone from the table, appeared to answer it, swore, and closed it. He walked to the bar, told Leo that his date had backed out and he would have another drink. Bar staff hear all sorts of tales of woe, and Leo listened while pretending to be interested and was about to pour another glass of red but was interrupted by a request to make it a large bourbon, instead.

Olivia pushed her glass forward to Oliver for attention and ordered a Manhattan. She was asked by the good-looking man if she would accept his offer to buy the drink. Olivia had played the game before and she declined. She would show no interest in the man. He had to play by her undisclosed rules. Then she nodded that she would accept one.

She turned her head away to watch her drink being prepared, she asked the barman what his name was, and when he said Leo she asked if that was his star sign. 'No, libra, the balance.' He replied.

She turned her attention back to Oliver, thanked him for the drink and the game progressed.

Leo was so smart that they should have named a cookie after him. He watched from a distance. Some people enjoy watching chess being played slowly and with well thought out moves. That was too sluggish for him. He was a spectator of a more gladiatorial contest. What he had observed was a forthcoming of the psychological tournament. In his mind, he called it, 'When Two Narcissists Collide.' It was played rarely enough in the bar but he enjoyed spotting the single players when they chose a target. Often he would act as the referee and arrange a good separation to help the intended victim. It was not appreciated that often when somebody he saw being love bombed, resented being saved. He was seen as the villain rather than Batman.

He had seen the opening gambits being played. No exchange of names, yet. The weakest would be the first to ask so that stories could be told about how wonderful that name was. Leo had also noticed that Oliver played the phone trick. He had pretended to get a call so that he could tell the barman, the innocent bystander, how he had been dumped. In reality he wanted to announce his availability to the good-looking woman at the bar.

She had played her trick of looking at her watch too often, frowning, checking her own phone for messages in order to say, more subtly, that she was missing her date.

Leo waited for the next move. The exchange of names. He laughed loudly inside when he heard that they had the same name in effect. 'Wonderful.' He thought. 'Here we go. The soulmate opening.'

The compliments flowed, their similarities discussed, their bad experiences with previous lovers. It was all going to plan. The ultimate goal was to capture the heart of the king, the defenceless piece that was protected by powerful supporters. They needed to isolate the other one's supporters and protectors. The queen was the one with real power and needed to be controlled.

Then they played 'small world, big lies' as they talked about being stood up because the person they were supposed to be meeting was not trusting and always accused them of cheating. 'I am not like that. I want to meet somebody who I can trust and who trusts me. I am tired of tricksters.

The next moves would be 'You are different to my usual type.' This was where he said he usually goes for blonds but your hair is lovely. May I touch it?' To which she would respond by saying that she liked clean shaven men but his stubble was very attractive.

It was all part of the soulmate opening being strengthened by placing the bishop in a defensive position allowing the castle to fortify a weakness.

The game moved to the point when they would find a more private and intimate place to continue the match of mismatch.

Leo knew that this one would end in a deadlock. Neither side would win and they would declare a draw with polite farewells and the declarations that they were not suited.

The reason being that both wanted to the dominant controller of the other and that was not going to happen.

'Stalemate.' Leo declared as Oliver returned to the bar, phone in hand, ready to go fishing again. His sarcasm went unnoticed.

Leo smiled at him and asked, 'More?'

'I always want more. Call me Oliver Twist.'

Leo said to himself, under his breath, 'I can see how twisted you are and she was as twisted as you. Stalemate is where neither win but this time, both of you lost because you are both losers.'

'Sorry my friend. Are you alright.'

Leo replied, 'Just lost in my thoughts.'

Oliver started talking. 'Didn't work out. Talked all the time. Wanted to control the conversation, a real control freak.'

Coincidentally, they were exactly the words Olivia was saying to Mark, the barman, as she positioned herself on the stool that allowed her to look at her reflection in the mirror. She flicked her auburn hair and settled down. The bar was just a few a few yards away down the road and she spotted a good-looking man sitting nearby. Mark had seen this so many times.

'That bastard has stood me up.' She said to Mark with her voice loud enough to be heard by her new target. She wanted a new game with a less practised opponent.

'Can I have some more, please?' she said as an invitation to be asked if the new man could buy her a drink.

And meanwhile, Oliver sat with his phone on the table of a

different lair. He let his eyes search for a suitable target. Then he picked up his aide and moved to the bar cursing about his disappointment.

Everything had gone full circle. He had walked another revolution of his life in somebody else's shoes only to find that they pinched. Time for a change of footwear.

WHO'S A PRETTY BOY?

Bill loved himself. When Emma first met him, he was so charming that she knew she had met her soulmate. She liked his designer stubble, his dark eyes and strong build. His clothes were always dark in color and he needed to wear brighter things, she thought. She adored him, and wanted to give him anything and everything that would make him happy and therefore, he would love her more and more. She was the opposite in looks to him. She was petite, blond and had a wonderfully smooth complexion that had no need for makeup. She was very beautiful.

Their first holiday together would be wonderful. It would end a few days before his birthday and to express her love, she wanted an exotic present for him. She thought long and hard. He had few friends apart from her and during their time together she had lost contact with most of hers. He did not like her mixing with other people. He had shown signs of jealousy even though she was devoted to him. That meant that they both felt lonely apart from when they were together.

Then, one day while she was buying some bits and pieces in the high street, she was stopped in her tracks outside a pet shop. In the window there was a big parrot. She went inside and chatted to the sales assistant who told her that the brightly decorated bird was a Macaw. He answered her questions about whether or not it would talk and, yes it would.

She thought it would be perfect for Bill because he would have company from something that he would not feel threatened by.

She bought the bird and the bits she would need to care for it. A cage, water and food bowls and a big mirror. It was all too much for her to carry and delivery was arranged for the following day. Bill would be out working and it would be his birthday surprise, although in advance.

When he got home, Emma had a smile on her face as he walked into the living room. The bird spread its feathers as if a threat had appeared.

'This is your birthday present, Bill. I thought it would keep you company when I am doing other things.'

'What other things are you going to do? Go out and meet other people, men, while I am occupied? Thank you but I do not want a bird in my life that will talk even more than you do when you just prattle on and on.' His tone was nasty and he walked out of the house.

Emma burst into tears and sobbed at her foolishness.

The next day he returned. 'Sorry about that but you should have thought it through.'

'Where did you go? Did you go home to your place?' Emma asked. He would go off for days at a time when it suited him without explanation. It was if he lived two lives. One with Emma and another in his secret world that was never to be talked about.

Before he could tell her some well-constructed lies, fate stepped in. 'Who's a pretty boy? Who's a pretty boy?' The macaw spoke.

This struck a nerve with Bill. A pet who could tell him how wonderful he was.

He warmed to the big bundle of pretty feathers and just said, 'We should give it a name. How about Bill junior because it has a big bill.' Emma laughed at the joke that she did not find funny but it was a sign that he had calmed down.

'Where did it learn to say that?' he asked.

'I taught him yesterday. I thought it would be good for him to tell you that you are so handsome and lovely. We should teach him more words to say.' Emma lied to him. The bird already knew those words but she was worried that Bill would get jealous of the person who had fed that sentence into Bill Junior's vocabulary.

22

Life returned to what seemed normal to them.

The birthday came and went and the season started to change from summer to the fall.

Bill Jr occupied himself by looking into the mirror and saying those complimentary words but Bill realised that the parrot was talking to himself. He had competition for the praise he needed. The mirror disappeared one day and ended up smashed in the bin.

'Jr broke the mirror with its big beak so I cleaned up the cage and we will get another one someday.'

With the mirror gone, Bill could once again hear the words that idolised him without the fear that they were being directed at a reflection.

He closed his eyes and prompted Jr to say the words he needed. When he opened them, he saw Jr looking at his reflection in the water bowl and he got angry.

Bill reached for the steel container and the bird grabbed his thumb with its huge claws as its beak dug into his finger.

'You ugly bastard.' Bill shouted as he removed his hand and slammed the cage door shut.

As if it knew the score, Jr kept on and on with the same new motto, 'You ugly bastard, you ugly bastard, you ugly bastard.'

The cover was thrown over the cage and the bird was silent. Bill explained the cuts on his hand as an accident while he was fixing the car. Emma believed him.

The words that Bill had taught him were repeated from time to time but Bill insisted that they were not from him and Jr must have learnt them when in the pet shop. 'Children do things like that. They get pleasure from being little shits.'

It was getting later in the year; the chill of November was making it necessary to dress warm. The cover for Jr's cage changed from a sheet to a blanket and Bill seemed to spend more

23

time away. Emma grew suspicious and suspected that his need for admiration was being topped up by others as she was feeling less romantic as his control was growing to extremes. He questioned what she did at work and although she worked in a small office doing bookkeeping, he wanted descriptions of everybody who also worked there. If she was late back then he would accuse her of going for drinks and extras with her boss who was old enough to be her father.

She thought long and hard about leaving her job so that Bill would appreciate what she was doing to please and satisfy him.

Bill spent hours preening himself more than Junior did. He would trim his eyebrows to his liking, use a strimmer on his stubble and balding head to maintain it at the length that made him look like a cowboy, moisturise his skin, shave his armpits and pubic hair so that he would have more hair on his face than the rest of his body.

He would leave the bathroom naked, find Emma and as if making fun would shout out, 'Who's a pretty boy, who's a pretty boy, who's a pretty boy.'

Emma smiled her admiration back at him. She had to be his mirror image so she shaved every hair off apart from her blond hair. He was the model maker.

She laughed too loudly when Junior added his words. 'You ugly bastard, you ugly bastard, you ugly bastard.'

Bill slapped the cage, got dressed and walked out with words directed to the macaw. 'You will pay for that.'

When Thanksgiving Day arrived, Emma told Bill that she was going to prepare a special dinner for them but, although he never cooked, he insisted that as it was a special day, he would prepare the meal. Emma was pleasantly shocked but also happy that he was making an effort for once. He insisted that as part of the

24

surprise, she should stay out of the kitchen.

'Is everything going to plan? Emma asked as she opened the door slightly and took a big sniff at the smells of roasting that greeted her.

'Yes indeed. I have put the blanket over Jr's cage to keep him quiet while I cook, by the way.'

There was something in his tone that made her suspicious. She lifted the blanket off Jr's cage and found it empty. 'Where is junior?' She shouted. 'He has escaped.'

'He is in here. I thought he needed warming up. It is a cold day. The food is nearly ready. Please set the table.'

Emma rushed into the kitchen and there on a carving dish was a roasted bird.

'That is not a turkey, that is Junior.' Emma was hysterical.

Bill pulled a leg off the carcass and started to eat it.

Emma screamed. 'You ugly bastard, you ugly bastard, you ugly bastard.' She repeated the words that she had heard Junior say to Bill that made him angry.

With that, Bill started to choke on a sharp bone. He collapsed onto the floor as he gasped for breath.

'Who's a pretty boy, now?' Emma muttered. He was wearing the red, yellow and blue sweat shirt she had bought him. As if the penny had dropped at last, she answered the question she had asked. 'Not you. You are an ugly and evil man who has been hurt by the beautiful creature that was truthful in what it said. I am glad it got its revenge. How the hell could you be jealous of a bird? You are bloody mad.'

She dialled 911, told the responder that her man had choked on his own words; laughed at the inappropriate joke, said sorry and waited for the ambulance to arrive.

She reached into Bill's pocket, took his keys and removed the one to her door, and returned the rest to his hand. She saw the scar that Junior had made with his beak and laughed again.

When they took him away, she told them to take him back to his place when they had treated him.

'He will never come back here again, ever.'

She put the remains of Junior into a box and buried him in the garden with a little cross. She would remember him with love but the other Bill would be forgotten in time. The love she thought she had rapidly turned to disdain and loathing.

Her thoughts about the wonderful man who changed into a monster made her wonder what might have happened if she had a child in the house rather than a parrot and she shuddered with fear.

HOOK, LINE AND SINKER

The earthworm is not the major player in this story. It was the bait, the false charm that is offered to catch the innocent but hungry fish. The attractiveness was important, Rod knew, and he spent time ground baiting the area of the lake where he had set himself up to snap up the biggest and prettiest catch he wanted.

Now, although the targets were mirror carp, the fish is not a major player in this story either, it was needed to satisfy the needs of the angler. They were attracted by the wriggling and dancing of the worms and they would approach cautiously, looked at what was tempting them. Then they would stop for a while appraising what was on offer, perhaps they swam away for a few moments before returning to take the bait.

The float bobbed. The angler struck. The fish was hooked and, as much as it fought, it was unable to dislodge the barbs that had pierced its mouth. Gradually it was hauled in, the hook removed and was put into a keep net where it could live but, as a prisoner.

The man, Rod, admired his catch but wanted more than he had. He replaced his fat body onto the seat next to his tackle box, wiped his slime covered hands dry and praised himself on his skills.

Another worm was put on the hook and cast into the water. Another fish was attracted, hooked and netted. One fish was big enough to feed many people, but he enjoyed pulling as many as he could from the lake. Today, he had caught three and they filled his keep net.

He thought that the fish in his net enjoyed being his possessions but they were scared and unable to be free. When a hand appeared and pulled one out by the gills, the other fish were jealous because that one must be the favourite and would be looked after and then returned to freedom, to swim away again with friends and to jump out of the water and then splash back in.

Life had been fun until they were trapped.

The fish was held up in Rod's arms as he posed for the photos he would keep. Being smart, or so he thought, he set his phone up to video what he had caught. A photo with a fish weighing 20lb was impossible to take but his triumph had to be put into his archive of selfies.

He laid the fish on the ground and did his best to use the big scales as a mirror, as the name implied. Almost as a punishment, it was left to die. Rod laughed as the fish gulped and squirmed as its life ebbed away.

It was then skinned, gutted, speared with a metal rod and placed over a fire to cook.

Rod wanted the total consumption of the life and flesh of his prey. He munched away, cursing every so often as he picked bones from his mouth with his fat and grubby fingers. Although the flesh tasted muddy, he wanted to be the big and strong predator who catches and devours.

Having caught his fill for the moment, he felt unable to return the rest of his prisoners and so he took them out one by one and discarded them on the bank to suffer. As he had caught them, they were his and their fate would be decided by him.

They would die and attract the flies that would lay their eggs and the during the following days would provide him with maggots to catch different fish that he needed in order to prove what a wonderful man he was in his ability to attract, catch and fling away those beautiful creatures that he had no feelings for. His belief was that they only existed to provide pleasure for him.

He sat for a while making comparisons in his head with various women he had known. The stories in his mind ran to a common theme. He would attract, catch and keep them shut in an emotional prison where they could not escape to find other men. He had a high opinion of himself, even with his over large belly and the women he attracted with his charm and flattery should have felt honoured to be chosen for his company. Like the fish, they were good to look at but they could not be trusted. Sooner or later they would abandon him, usually for a nicer man, in their stupid eyes, and he would have to find a replacement.

What he did with the fish was the best option. Once they had been caught then they needed to be dumped before they dumped him. Those fish were his symbols of women he had lost, and although he had not thought of killing or murdering them, because he would be forced to live his life in a jail, it was no offense to be rid of the spare carp he had taken from their place of comfort to a nylon prison until he chose to eliminate them from the world.

After he had left, an alligator left the water and moved towards the discarded fish. It consumed them one by one and crept off to sleep for a while.

The next day, Rod returned to the same spot, swore loudly that the previous day's bounty had disappeared. No maggots to use. He slumped to the ground to open his bag to retrieve his box of baits. This time, he would use peas and sweetcorn to catch the carp. Ground bait always worked for him. He sweetened the moment with tempting treats as if he was doing it for pleasing the fish. It was what he did with women. Sweet words to get them to like him and when the time was right, he would use a bigger and tastier bait to get them even closer. Then, bang, the line was pulled tight and the hook sank in. After that, they could not and would not escape. He could do with them whatever he wanted.

He was so engrossed with setting his traps that he did not notice the alligator approaching on its way to the place where it had found food the day before. It was a consumer of detritus.

It then caught and consumed what it knew was a big lump of rotten flesh. It dragged Rod into the lake. He screamed his last breaths as he was twisted and submerged in the grip of huge jaws.

29

The better predator and hunter had won. The alligator did what they do. They catch and consume for nourishment rather than for pleasure. They never sought the joys of trophy hunting or feeling macho at the control of their prey.

The fish that still lived in the lake were now able to nibble away on Rod's remains without any fear of being trawled.

There were no more hooks, no more lines, just one sinker; the poacher and controller of lives who was never found or even missed.

The predator of predators had taken him away.

THE TERRACOTTA ARMY

Christine was out walking in the fresh morning air when she came across the entrance to a path between the hills. It looked inviting so she followed the track. Green shrubs reflected the sunlight and they gave shelter from the strong breeze that was blowing.

In front of her, glistening in the sunshine, she saw a handsome man who seemed to be a statue made from terracotta. She stood back and admired its looks and body shape.

'If I could only find a real man like you.' She declared to the wonderous figure in front of her.

To her great surprise it spoke back. 'You are beautiful and have a wonderful figure.' The mouth moved to speak those words. Then it started to open up like a Russian doll.

'I am so pleased to meet you. I think we have a lot in common. You enjoy walking in the countryside. So do I. Do you like the wild flowers around us?'

She nodded that she did.

'So do I. I love them. And do you like early sunrises?'

She shook her head to say that she did not. 'I prefer to stay in bed in the morning.' She replied.

'So do I.' the clay figure was now turning into an animated man.

'Do you like singing?' Christine was asked.

'Yes I do. I am a trained soprano.'

The reply was predictable. 'You know. I love opera and especially powerful voices.' His smile was overwhelming. 'We have so much in common.'

Then, another man seemed to appear from the original statue.

'I should tell you that you cannot use your phone here. There is no signal. May I have a look at it to see if I can help.'

She handed her phone over and he ran his thumb over the keys to see who she had been contacting in the past. He muttered words in a low angry voice and the phone turned to rock.

A third man suddenly started speaking. 'You are not as attractive as we first thought. You are lucky that we can tolerate ordinary people.' He had a sneer on his face.

And so it went on. A terracotta army of identical looking figures was now blocking her way. They all looked the same but their attitudes were different, although each and every one of them wanted to control her.

One by one, they took turns in insulting her looks, her height, the colour of her hair, her makeup, her choice of clothes and her lack of understanding about how they felt.

Christine was confused. What had started as one handsome and solid man had split into many. She decided that these other beings were really the different characteristics of the wonderful person she had first met. He was not a loving man but a complex of different trapping and controlling traits. She needed to escape but her road was closed.

She had a choice to make. To put up with what was happening or to bide her time while thinking about how she would get away. For her it was as if an avalanche of malevolent rocks had tumbled down.

Then she realised that clay models are brittle and would crack and crumble easily if they thought that they were losing the command they thought they had.

From frustration, Christine started screaming.

'STOP that now.' A loud voice ordered.

She screamed again and used her voice to lift the noise to her highest note. She would rather die as an opera singer than be killed by these manipulating monsters.

As she held the note, the clay started to crack. It started to fall apart and hit the ground as dust. She took a deep breath and sang again.

She climbed over the pile and moved forward to escape. Rain began to fall, gently at first and then more heavily. As she looked back, the dust was reforming into balls. Rather than being afraid that the original man would re-emerge, she walked back, fearless this time.

Her laughter echoed off the cliff walls until it was as if she was surrounded by copies of her happy and free self.

The reason she was laughing was that the balls of clay and mud stuck together in such a way that they no longer resembled a man but they looked like piles of horse shit.

'Got it right this time.' She spoke to the invisible piece of magic that had helped her to realise that not all that glistens is gold.

AH! SOUL MATES

They had so much in common. He thought he was handsome, funny, a good lover and an all round nice man. So did she.

Elaine, twenty seven years old with a good figure and bobbed blond hair, met David on a dating app and after a few weeks of chatting on WhatsApp, they had arranged their first date at a nice restaurant near her house. He gave her masses of compliments and told her that he loved short blond hair as he ran his fingers through it.

Soon after, they started making frequent love and he declared his love for her.

She was a divorcee who had left her husband after she had found out that he was cheating on her. He had been upset but put his hands up and had confessed. Elaine knew that she had been too occupied with her nursing job and so their love life had suffered from a mixture of fatigue and late night shifts.

After two more dates David moved in to Elaine's apartment that she bought with the money she got from the divorce.

She was hooked. This was the man for her. She had found her soul mate and he told her that he had found his. Alan had been a waste of space and time.

They enjoyed each other at first but Elaine felt pressured to do what was asked of her. Even though she would get back from work in the early hours, she was told to shower and get into bed and provide pleasure for David. It was fun at the beginning, she felt almost naughty like a girl in her first real romance. After a while the fun for her stopped and she tried to resist him. He then started becoming angry when she did not do what he wanted and threatened to leave her on more than one occasion. She had to hold on. Her marriage had failed and she needed to avoid losing another man. His grip was tightening and she felt she was being controlled by the man he had become.

Alan was a gentle soul who felt lonely after six years of marriage that had started well and then began to slip down a slippery slope of neglect and indifference. He had tried his best to keep her happy but there was something about her that he was unable to put his finger on. Rather than give up, Alan talked about starting a family but Elaine was worried about the commitment it would mean. A child would be the solution if the marriage was strong but would be a hindrance to happiness if it did not get better.

The affair that Alan had was a brief one. He chatted often to Marion during office hours. They were both employed by a company that made and sold car accessories. They were both at the same level in middle management and they talked about anything other than their jobs and the company they worked for.

Elaine and Marion had met at social gatherings organised by the company and although they were polite to each other, they never really bonded. Elaine found Marion a bit shallow and boring.

After a while, it was fairly obvious to Alan and his workmate that they were fond of each other and evening meetings were arranged when Elaine was working. In a predictable way, over time they progressed from bars to restaurants to Marion's bed.

Alan felt guilty that he was getting his sexual needs fulfilled by cheating. Love never entered his head, he loved Elaine too much. What he had was a physical relief but for Marion, it was more. She wanted to feel that Alan was emotionally attached to her and hinted that she would like them to be honest, tell his wife and then be together for ever.

They had known each other for a few years by the time the affair had started and had grown into a relationship that was ill balanced. He wanted a sexual partner and she wanted and needed a life partner. The two needs were incompatible. Alan told Marion it had to end and so it did. She could not understand it, after all she had thought that they were soul mates.

Hell hath no fury like a woman scorned and so Marion told Elaine what had been going on in the hope that there would be a divorce and Alan would come back to her as a result.

The divorce was set in motion but Marion did not achieve her goal. The plan did not work. Alan and Marion continued working together but their relationship reverted back to being colleagues rather than lovers.

So, here we are. Elaine was lonely as was Marion and Alan but the three of them were at a great distance. When Alan heard from a friend that Elaine had met somebody, he was upset. He asked for his name in case he knew him but he had no friends or acquaintances called David.

Alan, although not a stalker, wanted to know what this new man was like so he visited his old home that was owned by his ex-spouse and hid away until he saw a man let himself in. He took photographs on his phone to look at later and also took pictures of the man's car. As could be expected, Alan found no reason to admire his looks and he felt confused by his ex wife's choice.

Marion, thirty years old with long brunette hair, started using dating apps to find a companion who she could share requited love with. She was careful and made her choices with thoughtfulness. She had heard stories about what can go wrong.

Marion and Martin met on a dating app and after a few weeks of chatting on WhatsApp, they had arranged their first date at a nice restaurant near her house. He gave her masses of compliments and told her that he loved long brunette hair as he ran his fingers through it.

That went well and after the next date, they went back to her place for a romantic love making session. She was hooked. This was the man for her. She had found her soul mate and he told her that he had found his.

Alan had been a waste of space and time.

Alan thought about starting again with Marion. She had moved to a different branch in another town and made his move during a coffee break. He telephoned her with the intention of inviting her out for a drink. She was flattered but told him that she had met somebody else who was the love of her life. She told Alan that his name was Martin and he worked for local government in a role where he helped to administer various departments. She did not want to give his surname.

Alan had a lot of time on his hands and decided to research the two men who had won the ladies he had known in his life.

He found nobody in local government called Martin even though he searched the internet and phoned the reception of the big office.

He was not a stalker, as said before, but his curiosity was in need of answers. He, once again, wanted to see who was considered a better choice than himself.

It was Thursday and he complained that he had a cold coming, finished work early, drove near Marion's house and watched from behind a hedge. After about an hour or so, she drove into her drive, got out of her car and walked to the door. He waited for another hour before he gave up and returned to his car and drove back to the small apartment that was now his home after losing so much money in the split-up with Elaine.

He ate a small meal and then drove back to Marion's place. It was dark now and after another long wait, he saw a car pull up next to hers.

A man got out and Alan took photographs with the light from a street lamp. The man unlocked the door and rushed into the house. The bedroom light went on for a few moments before it was dimmed. Alan had seen enough. He got into his car, drove back to his place and poured himself a large drink, and then another.

He woke on the Friday morning with a hangover. He would miss work and transfer the pictures he had taken onto his laptop for a better view.

The pictures he taken the night before just showed the mystery man from the back so his face was not visible. What he did notice was the car. It was the same model as he had seen at Elaine's house. He brought up the pictures he had taken before but the registration number was obscured.

He jumped into his car and sped to Marion's house. The car was still in the drive. The numbers matched the ones of those he had taken at Elaine's place. He wanted to knock on the door and confront the man, but he thought he had no claim on his ex mistress. He had dumped her and she had found a new man. There again, he felt protective and he wanted to tell her that her new man was possibly a cheat.

He got into his car and drove to his old house and ex wife. He was going to tell her what he had found but she was out, possibly at work. Perhaps she had changed her shifts. As he was turning his vehicle around, David's or Martin's car drove up. He, whatever he was called, got out, let himself in as if he owned the place.

Alan needed to let two women know the truth. He tried phoning Elaine but she had blocked his number as instructed. She would be at the hospital, so he drove there to be told she was no longer working there. She had left her job to spend more time with her family, she had put it.

Like a mad delivery man, Alan drove to Marion's but she was out, her car had gone. He drove to Elaine's again. Her car was there but the other one was not.

He knocked on the door but there was no reply. He was now

lost for what to do so he drove to the office where Marion now worked, walked in, asked for her but she was on holiday, he was told.

On his way home he stopped at a red light. A car, the car, took a left turn from the adjoining side road on the green light. Alan put his foot down, jumped the lights and slowly followed his target. It made a few turns and eventually stopped. Alan drove past, pulled over and walked back to see whoever he was at that moment, open a door to be greeted by a red headed woman who grabbed him, kissed him and almost pulled him inside with cries of 'daddy's home' to the two young children who were as excited as their mother.

After a while when Alan had tracked his two exes down, he told them about the man in their lives, to Elaine, David Martin and to Marion, Martin David. They were upset, not happy but that was because they accused Alan of trying to wreck their relationship with a wonderful and caring man who would never cheat because he loved them. Both women claimed him as their soul mates. 'More like soul mites that suck you blood and leave you itching with irritation.'

The response he got from both of them was, 'you are the only thing that irritates in my life. Goodbye.'

He had a fleeting thought about visiting the house where he had seen yet another victim with the children, but decided against it.

He was frustrated that he could not help the casualties of this serial killer of emotions and hope. He was annoyed with himself that he could not come up with a solution.

He wrote the same words on two separate notes and posted them to Elaine and Marion. It simply said;

'Remember, he is NOT after you for you. He wants you for himself.' The big red letters might make them think.

He was never unblocked, never contacted and after Marion had left her job, he had no idea where she had gone. It was the same with Elaine.

The only answer Alan had was to blame himself for all that had gone wrong.

ONLY WEEDS GROW DURING A DROUGHT

Liam was taking advantage of the good weather. He was in the garden plucking weeds from his flower beds. Most of the plants he had set out in the spring had withered after the blazing sunshine had caught them. He had been unable to water them because there were restrictions on the use of his hose pipe during the drought. He cursed at the waste of his effort and at the ending of the only decorations he had in his life these days.

He was lonely and spent time on dating apps looking for the love of his life. His drought was the same as for his plants. Women he had met before were all short term loves who had left him. He was not bad looking he thought. He earnt a good salary and lived in a fairly attractive house. He thought he was the perfect catch. He could chat, he had interests that were normal rather than restrictive and it was about time he found somebody who would want to share their life with him. He had quite a few friends and they would meet up now and then to drink some beers and to watch a match.

After a few attempts on the app, he made contact with Julie. She looked good in her pictures and when they got to talking, it seemed she had the same interests as him. The chats got longer and longer until they decided that they were so much alike, they should meet up for a drink and maybe dinner.

When the evening came, they both recognised each other from the many video calls they had shared and with a kiss on the cheek, Julie sat at the bar and, when asked, ordered her drink.

The evening went well and another meeting was arranged. This time it would be at her house and she would cook dinner. Delighted at the progress, Liam bought some new clothes, a small gift for Julie and counted off the days until they would meet.

She looked good when she answered the door, invited him in

and enjoyed the compliments she got for the aromas of food that were wafting into his nose.

She poured some wine and started to talk. This time, rather than conversation, it was almost an interrogation about his past loves and their current status in his life. She wanted to know about his friends and family before she suggested that they went upstairs to make love. 'It is always better on an empty stomach.' She said.

The questioning continued about his favourite position, his best love making events, how he was able to satisfy his lovers and so on. The balance of conversation was one sided. She would avoid his questions by interrupting and asking her own, almost incessantly.

The irony hit him when she told him that they had so much in common when, after all, she had got to know about him whereas he knew nothing more about her than when he had first arrived.

She talked and talked about herself. How she had been let down by previous boyfriends and how they had always cheated on her.

Eventually they ate but without appetites for anything other than her lust for knowledge.

He stayed over and, in the morning, went to work.

The phone calls and messages started.

'Are you OK?

'Did you enjoy our evening?

'Are you around later?'

They went on and on to interrupt his work schedule and when he decided not to respond, then her onslaught became more oppressive.

The messages became demanding of his time and attention and she told him that they had to meet later to talk.

Waiting to be dumped again, Liam was puzzled by the speed at which everything had happened and the intensity of her needs.

When they met up at her house, she was apologetic and went on and on again about previous men who had taken advantage of her good nature.

They made up and made love. She explained that she needed to know where he was through the day and that in order to make things work he should postpone meetings with his pals and family so that they could get to know each other better.

Liam should have been happy, he knew. He was staying with Julie more than he was at home. They spent a lot of time just chatting with her doing most of the talking. They made love, but with her taking the lead to ensure that she got the most pleasure and blamed him when she was not satisfied with his efforts.

When the rows started, she wanted him to leave and stay away. Then she would ask him to come back. When he did she started to soft soap him again and did her best to explain small details about herself such as small scratch marks on her back and the bedroom smelling different to before.

He missed the contact with his drinking mates and wanted to have an evening out with them. She forbade him to do so, threatening that she would start telling people what a bad lover he was and how he had cheated on her.

'Who would you tell? We have no shared friends or family. It would fall on deaf ears.'

'But you have a boss, you have work colleagues who would not appreciate you hitting me.'

'I never did.'

She showed him some bruises that she had on her thigh. 'I can show them this.' She snapped a picture on her phone and sent it to him.

He was trapped. Blackmailed for something he had not done, wondering who had, and life was miserable. He was in a jail with her being the prison governor.

At work the next day, he asked for a meeting with his boss. She sat him down and asked him if he had problems. His work had dropped in standards and he seemed to be distracted a lot of the time.

Taking a deep breath, he started his story from the beginning and told her about the threats that were being made.

Charlotte laughed and laughed. Liam was embarrassed and stood up to leave.

'Sit down.' His boss commanded. 'We need to have a talk about the birds and the bees.'

'I am not a child.' He started to stand up again.

'What you have described is something that happened to me but with a man, obviously.' She started. Do you have a photo of this woman?' She asked out of curiosity rather than anything else.

Liam showed her a couple of pictures. Charlotte burst out laughing again.

'Small world, Liam. This is one of the women my partner was involved with. She had her hooks into him and he had his into her. It would never work. Two control freaks fight for the big red button to press and so they ended up walking away from each other for ever. He found others to build his world and so I walked away from him, cut all contact and started to be free again. That is what you will do. Walk away, ignore the threats, they are lies to control you.'

Liam breathed deeply and thanked Charlotte.

'Now you can get back to your gardening. When all that happened to me, my mother knew that I had been lonely and had grabbed the first offer I got. She said something that you should know as well. Only weeds grow during a drought. When it rains again, so the beauty and nice people will come back into your life.'

Charlotte smiled and blew him a friendly kiss. She would have been perfect had she not been his boss, he thought.

46

BAITING APPS

Applying for a job is straightforward. You find a vacancy, apply, fill in a form with your details and qualifications, submit it, get an interview to assess your suitability, judge what is on offer and then accept or decline that offer if it suits you. Candidates are interviewed, vetted for their appropriateness for what is required.

You might exaggerate your skills and the company might over enhance what is being promised. It is necessary for both parties to know the truth.

Oh, sorry. This was supposed to be about dating apps where human resources can become inhuman supplies. To be fair, and to avoid complications, not all dating apps are run for profit. Some might be based on a real desire to introduce lonely people to each other.

Companies search for people who will fulfil a role that will benefit both the employee and employer. Yet, the very words give a lot away. The employee is the person used to benefit the employer, the boss. Some, actually, most companies are ethical and honest but there are some that exploit rather than employ their staff.

They will make promises that will not be kept to get somebody on board. They will find out what the applicant wants and offer that to entice. If the job seeker is good at creative skills, that is what the company wants. If the expertise is in number crunching, then…

Imagine what is the reality of a predator, a narcissist, on the prowl on dating apps. They want to find the most suitable prey for their needs. He or she does not have to be weak, stupid or unable to work out what could happen. The predator is skilled in his methods. He has to hide in the undergrowth to get into the

47

underwear. He is charming, caring, sharing and all the time he is looking at your CV. He will discover your likes and dislikes, your hobbies, your family connections, your previous experience and he will then make up his mind about your suitability for the job of being his supplier of attention, praise, bewilderment and love.

Once you have the job then the conditions will change. He will demand rather than ask, he will make threats rather than reward. And if you threaten to resign, then he will look for other candidates to take your place.

The problem is that you have signed a binding contract. You have the need and desire to please the boss even though he has many faults.

The terms of employment you have agreed to, even against your better judgement is that you belong to the company, the boss, twenty-four hours per day, seven days per week and you are not allowed to make or receive personal phone calls, text messages and social media contact with anybody other than the boss.

He will expect you to be ready to receive his calls even when he goes out for 'business meetings' and to be ready for him when he gets back.

You will always be too busy to contact family members and friends because you need what he gives. He will pay you a few compliments and show affection in return for the huge profits his ego makes from your efforts to please.

OK, enough of all that. You have the strength to resign, to walk out the door and shut it firmly behind you. You can decide when to squash the mosquito that is happily sucking blood from your arm. It is only benefitting itself with no return for you other than fear and dread that you will lose the false imitation of love that you wanted. There is real and unconditional love out there when you look carefully. Perhaps you look for it in different ways or you are more selective in the dating apps you use and in the approach of the people who you make contact with. You are looking for a partnership rather than an employer of your emotions for their benefit.

The sad truth is that people go for the same thing again, even after they have been caught before. It is as if they are still attracted to the lies, exaggerations and grooming of the person who wants to invest a small amount of affection and charm in order to reap the harvest of attention, admiration and sacrifice.

Be very cautious and retain your sense of pride and self-respect. Steer clear of the dangerous hunters of emotional feed.

In short, there are dating apps than can become baiting apps when they are used by nasty and self-centred predators.

SMOKE AND MIRRORS

Magic is illusion, deception and the misleading manipulation of the audience of one or more people.

Great performers are artists who the audience know are clever at their craft. Everybody who buys a ticket knows that they will see something which is deceiving them for entertainment.

Tom was an illusionist who performed his tricks to his selected admirers. He had learnt how charlatans had devised a way to convince people that he could conjure up spirits by the reflection of projecting images onto a thin haze of smoke.

He never used smoke or mirrors, he used his skills of deception to groom women into thinking they were in love with him to the extent that they would do anything to keep him, to maintain his illusion that they believed in.

One part of the mystery was that he did not know how he did it. He deceived while thinking that he was being honest but, behind the distortions of reality that he created, there was a man who was so selfish that he believed that his magic was genuine.

It was if he had been programmed into behaving in set ways, as if he worked to a plan in his mind that was not his thinking. He had one motive, to feel good by being told he was wonderful, by controlling others and to be placed high on a throne where people would fall at his feet and beg for his love that he would not requite, but which he pretended that he did…at a price.

In the early days of smoke and mirrors, the projector light was provided by oil with a wick which flickered. The images that people saw looked spooky as a result and added to the effect. Tom was also an unstable and shimmering light that shone with a brilliant flame sometimes, but also dimmed and faded so that the audience of one, two or three women would want the illumination of the picture of Tom to glow again. To do that, they had to be involved in his repeat of the first sessions of charm. Then they needed to be even more deeply in love, more devoted, more subjected to his demands.

It was all so similar to the genie in the lamp who appeared in a puff of smoke, smartly dressed and with promises that wishes would be fulfilled. However, genies are not good friends, apparently. Some like to torment those who seek to free them from being trapped in their psychological lamp or bottle.

Genies are not there to help people at all. They want to be the boss. They make demands for loyalty and subservience because they are the ones with the powers of magic.

The genie arrives in smoke and Tom pretended to be a genie who provided the solutions that are needed for those outside the lamp. The truth is that Tom exchanged being trapped in the lamp of misery at not being adored for the imprisonment of those who caressed it, cared for it, and did what was demanded of them.

The way to escape the deception and hurt is to open windows, let the smoke blow away and turn the projector off. The fantasy might have seemed good and the temptation is to keep it going, but at a cost. Hallucinations are never more real than dreams. When the recipients of the wonderful illusions created by the smoke and mirrors wake up, the dream is lost.

Perhaps it was a nightmare after all. It was a distraction from the truth, the stalking chameleon. The thing you are better off without. After all, you were not the only person rubbing his lamp and wishing.

HARRY THE HYPNOTIST

Harry was a theatre hypnotist. He would perform for money and for benefits. He walked onto his set dressed in black. He had a confident swagger and would build his act by using simple tricks that were aimed at creating a belief that he had special powers over the audience.

He would test the volunteers that he asked for with an apparent check on their ability to be put into a trance. Known only to himself, he also gauged their suitability for manipulation both on and off the platform.

He used shortcuts to find women. He wanted them to accept his suggestions and to act out what he wanted them to do.

The camouflage was generated by him choosing male and female participants but as the process moved on, he would make the men do foolish things such as having a conversation with a doll, proposing to and kissing it.

Of course, the crowd loved it. There is something about humans that amuses them at somebody else's expense.

He continued to develop the sense of control over minds that his performance was built on.

Then he would target the women he had no desire for and with a tap on the shoulder, they would become another entertainment for the gathering. He would whisper something into their ear and on cue, they would become the focus of delight for the onlookers.

And so it went on. One by one, the contributors to the show were asked to give their names and what they did for a living. He used and then dismissed them to a huge round of applause until there would be one man and a woman left.

The woman would be the next to delight the mob who looked on as if they were hungry watchers of mayhem in a Roman arena waiting for the gladiators to slaughter each other.

'What is your name, my dear.'

'Susan' she responded in a shy way waiting for instructions that would make others laugh and potentially embarrass her.

Harry whispered into her ear, as he had done with the others. Susan stood up and danced around as if she was a ballerina. After the loud cheering and clapping she was returned to her seat.

George, the remaining man spoke to the audience in an address as if he were the President. It was satirical and funny as Harry had figured that George had no love for the man who ran the country.

Harry took his bows, went backstage, drank some bourbon and walked out to the car park. He unlocked his camper van and waited.

Susan had been out with her friends that evening. The four of them had all come in their own cars and after talking about the show and how much they had enjoyed it, they said their farewells and went their separate ways. Susan was a single woman who had been cheated on by men in her past and she was happy that she had spent time with company she liked and without having to explain anything to anybody when she got home. She felt that she had been nothing more than a magnet for bad guys who wanted to explore her shapely body and who, having had their fun, walked away. She felt that she had been nothing more than a beautiful butterfly who attracted collectors who would admire her and then pin her body to a board as a happy memory to be looked at from time to time. She was tired of such hoarders of innocence.

Harry would be different. He had told her that she was beautiful and he would treat her with kindness. She was sure she had found the perfect man as she got into the back of his van.

Harry touched her shoulder and spoke into her ear.

She was so convinced that, as she undressed ready to make love, it felt so natural. Other guys had to wait for two or three dates before any intimacy happened, but with this perfect man, it would have been foolish to hang on for the polite timing. It would happen now.

Harry was the best lover she had ever had. He was so handsome and charming. She was besotted to the extent where she noticed but ignored his fat belly, bad breath and his lack of sexual interest in her but just for his own orgasm.

Her infatuation was extreme. He was magnificent and she wanted to marry him, spend her life with him, have children and be happy ever after.

She even believed his story about why she had seen panties and a bra beside the bed. 'It was a joke my friend played on me because I have always been a faithful partner. Some folks just do not trust me because I am attractive to women but I ignore all that. I have been looking for my perfect mate and that is you.'

He got dressed and told her to find her car and make her way home. He took her number and promised that he would call the next day.

Susan waited and waited but she received no calls at all. In desperation, she assumed she had written it down wrong and that he must be so anxious that he could not contact her.

She booked a ticket for his performance that would happen in two days time. She sat in her seat and when he arrived on the stage and asked for volunteers, she almost ran to the stage. When Harry saw her, he tapped her on the shoulder and whispered in her ear. She returned to her seat, relieved that she had not participated in his performance.

She had forgotten all about his last one. What she did notice this time, when she went onto the stage and he had whispered to her, was his tubby belly and his horrible halitosis. 'Thank goodness I'm not his girlfriend.' She whispered to herself.

Susan never knew where she had lost her panties and bra a few nights before.

After the performance and having sex with the evening's female accessory he had chosen, he added the newly acquired underwear to his collection like a butterfly collector with his new kill.

This had started with the clients he had abused when he was a hypnotherapist. The name he was given when he was exposed was hypno-the-rapist by the local newspaper but sadly, no charges were ever brought against that monster who loved the power of suggestion he had over his victims for his self pleasure and ego boosting.

BIG BALLS

Nobody knew who was who. They were massed into the ball room and the air was full of the mixture of perfumes and sweat. Masked balls were a nightmare for those assisting the gentry who were attending.

The duties that they had for their masters and mistresses were so similar. The application of costumes and in some cases girdles and corsets. The brushing out and powdering of wigs, finding shoes with big heels to build an illusion of height, and for the men cod pieces to make their genitals look more ample than they actually were.

Cleavages for the women had to be wide, deep and attractive in order to get attention as the guests were arriving, mincing in on their squashed and angled feet.

The mirror balls were revolving flashing light onto the mirrors that covered the walls. All angles were covered to show off the magnificence of the costumed, mask wearing thrill seekers.

The ball was about to begin. The conversations in Venice were about who was who and who would be with who for fun when wine was drunk and encounters would be made. They were hiding their identities because what they were going to do clashed with the church's rules of abstention from meat to eat, that is, and religious abstention from carnal pleasures.

The masks were an early way of doing what is described as hiding in public. They also hid the ugly from the beautiful, the old from the young and the better off from the poorer attendees.

Ornate masks were the outward means of stating the worth of the wearer along with the extravagance of the gowns and the amount of gold leaf applied to both.

In this way in the 16th century, strangers would meet for sex without having to know who it was with but the benefit for some was that if everything was good, then the masks could be slipped off and the real identity exposed.

Some women would rush away in horror when they saw the faces pock marked from sexually transmitted diseases and vice versa.

Beneath the mask the façade was seen for real. Some of the men enjoyed using the balls for having same gender sex, others used their wealth and power to hurt what had now become their captives for sadistic words and acts.

The advantage of being able to take part in an orgy and then walk away was immense. Wives, husbands and churchmen, maybe nuns, could indulge themselves in total privacy although they were in public.

Nearly everybody won apart from the poor sufferers of abuse and who lost their confidence in themselves that would be long lasting after the balls had ended.

To be loved is one thing, to be used is another. To be charmed by a man or woman hiding behind a mask is wonderful. To discover what there was underneath could and would be horrific after the intimacy of the moment was nothing more than rape.

The question with those people is, were they acting the fool or was it a fool acting?

Venice was a rich city, a centre of trade and it attracted the wealthy whose riches in turn appealed to prostitutes and thieves. It was also a place where malaria killed people and so the urge to live life to the full while people still had some before possible death, was a driving force. Equally the need to indulge customers in nights of rampant erotic behaviour was important to the traders. The fact that they could do what they wanted while wearing a disguise was a fantastic incentive to take part and they would only be known by the people who could pressure sell to them afterwards.

The idea of masked balls was such a good one for the partakers that they were held all over Europe and the Americas.

We should assume that such things have stopped happening. The idea of sex without responsibility has survived through history and still happens. The rich can afford masks and grand costumes but for others, the masks have to be created by the use of words to charm, to entice and to hide the person behind it.

And we all know who that involves.

DEADEYE DICK

Richard was a marksman, an assassin and a hunter. He was an expert at hiding himself and being able to blend in with the crowd but he had one aim, to select his targets and to pick them off one by one; or more if the opportunity arose. He did not kill people; his goal was to capture emotions from others that would build his own sense of self-worth and to bolster his ego.

He had a huge arsenal of weapons, a pistol for short range strikes, a rifle for medium range attacks and a sniper rifle for longer distances.

The first thing that was done was reconnaissance, getting to know about the objective and to define his coordinates for the next stage, the strike. This was always done in a subtle and gentle way to avoid frightening his prey away. It was easier to shoot a sitting duck rather than one that was flying away.

He used a wide range of ammunition that included the 'if you like something, then I love it' bullet. That had a good effect at any range and was designed to bring the target closer. That was his favourite for disguising his onslaughts. It brought his objective into a sharp focus for using his 'compliment and charm rounds' which had the objective of reducing defences. This was his anaesthetic dart before he closed in with his, 'we have so much in common we must be soulmates' was the next shot.

He worked through a whole belt of ammo until he had captured his choice and then used training techniques to get compliance, control and obedience by weakening the will power of his admirers.

Where he thought he was extra clever was instead of pursuing one goal, he had a wide range of vision so that if he missed one then, he would select another or more. It made no difference whether or not he had a single person or lots in his sights. He wanted to recruit a whole army of loyal and faithful followers.

He wants to capture hearts and mould his victims into the shape he wants them to have. He needs their undying love to feed him until he has picked them dry and when they have nothing left, threatens them to give the 'more' that they are unable to provide.

The lucky ones escaped by refusing to give in to his demands, to recognise the huge value they had and the no value he was to them.

Their metaphorical heads are displayed on the wall in his mind that recall his victories over the innocent who managed to bite the bullet and revive their lives after the predator had been dismissed.

Thinking about all this, it is no wonder they called Richard; Deadeye Little Dick. That is what he was and is.

NO STRINGS ATTACHED

Martin had been a landscape gardener when Sophie was born. He had been a fighter pilot in his earlier days. Fast jets were the love of his life. The thrill he got at being propelled through the sky was irreplaceable. He would screech high into the clouds and swoop low over fields and trees that were so close; but the control was in his hands.

He had flown in the Vietnam war. His life had been dangerous but the stories were always thrilling to hear.

Sophie, his granddaughter, would sit on his knee when she was young and would listen to his tales, although they were watered down to avoid the violence and savagery of conflict and bloodshed.

He would always end his stories with the line, 'You know, I always wore a parachute. I never used it but it gave me security.'

After the war he became a commercial pilot ferrying people from place to place. He enjoyed meeting the passengers and talked with them as he walked down the aisle between the seats and chatted, answered questions and appreciated the respect he was given by the folk whose lives were temporarily in his hands and those of his co-pilots.

The fun was severely diluted when security increased and he found that he was locked away in the cabin with one other person and contact with his human load was reduced to zero.

As she grew up she heard more stories from him about his times in the corporate world and how the enemy was always better hidden than the ones he had fought in the war. His words were always analogous to the fights he had.

'The boss I had would smile at you while he was working away to remove you as competition. I never knew why. I was not pushing for promotion, I just wanted to last long enough to retire

63

with a pension. He would snipe and shoot his lies out behind my back. I knew that one day he would shoot me down because he had bigger firepower than me. So, waiting for that day, I studied landscape gardening. When I was on a wait-over in some city or another, I would look at gardens big and small to inspire me in planting trees and flowers so that if, and when, it happened and I was finally shot down, I had my parachute to float me into safety.'

It was not too long after her grandfather died that Sophie was drawn into the life of a charming man who told her how beautiful she was and how they were so suited for each other.

He was different to her other boyfriends who although they had treated her with respect, lacked the words that she wanted to hear, but had not realised until Jeremy oozed charm, compliments and words of love. She fell for him and accepted that he had a history of mistrust from others in his life. She wanted to help him to recover from all that hurt he had suffered. This meant that she would have to be there for him a lot. He was insecure and he pushed the romance ahead at a speed which surprised her. Sophie was head-over-heels with her new love; a real love and she did her best to please him.

One day, Sophie visited her grandmother who was lonely after her Martin's death. Still a beautiful woman, made up and dressed as if her husband would return from flying all over the world, she started to reminisce about her brave hero of a husband who had become bored with life after the excitement of flying fast and low in combat had been replaced by a routine that was controlled by others.

She choked a little with the emotion of her loss but said, 'He was at his happiest when he pulled on the rip cord and floated away from the corporate jet into the gardens of his dreams which he built for others to enjoy. As he always said; everybody needs a parachute, just in case.'

Those words were repeated to Sophie, but almost as if her much loved grandfather was saying them.

When Sophie was with her gran, her phone kept on pinging. It was Jeremy asking, demanding to know, where she was. She messaged back to explain where she was and why, but the pinging continued every two or three minutes.

She told her grandmother that it was her partner and he was being caring by checking she was safe.

'Sophie, you know I love you very much as did grandad. May I ask you a few questions about him, whoever he is, please?'

Sophie nodded her approval as she said, 'Jeremy', in response.

The white-haired lady started. 'I met your granddad during the war. He was away for long periods of time. I did not call him every minute to check that he was alive and well. I never worried that he spent his time in the brothels in Saigon because I knew he would never even thing of doing that. I trusted him. Yes, he was a handsome and charming man who always had a mountain of compliments to give me that made me feel special but I never, ever thought for a moment that he did that to receive words back that would please him. What seems to be happening is that your Jeremy is giving you a box of chocolates that he wants to eat himself. Beware, my precious young lady. Something does not feel right to me. There is care and there is control. Check that your chute has been well prepared and is safe.' She winked as a piece of punctuation calling her advice to an end.

After hugging and smiling together, Sophie started her drive home. She did not want to think about parachutes. She was, above all, looking forward to seeing Jeremy at home, having a drink, making love and cuddling up on the couch.

He was sitting down when she got back. He remained fixed in place without a smile and with his fists clenched.

Without quoting what was said word by word, it suffices to

say that the insults and accusations flew at Sophie as thick and fast as the bullets her grandfather had been on the receiving end of, and although she tried every attempt to miss being struck, the words hurt her as much as rounds of ammunition. She was about to crash as her dreams shattered around her. He was showing himself to be the enemy who had been camouflaged and hidden behind the charming screen. He was the male version of the sirens who lured sailors to their death on the rocky shores in the myth.

She shouted at him to leave and after his threats and protests that she was being stupid because she loved him, he stormed out.

She blamed herself for damaging their relationship and wanted to call him to ask for forgiveness.

She wanted to chat to her friends about the great love she had and how it should progress after the big row. There were none that she could think of. He had removed them with surgical precision. She had put distance between herself and her friends as demanded for the 'good' reasons he had explained about the time and attention she gave them would damage the relationship she had with him, because after all, soul-mates needed to be together and in constant contact every hour of everyday, except when he was away on business, and then he would call her when convenient.

It was the same with her parents and siblings. After being charmed by Jeremy, they were pushed further and further into a less than frequent part of her life. They had liked him and thought it was just a sign that she was happy with the best man she had ever met.

She wanted to shower to freshen up but she was not sure which clothes to wear afterwards. She thought about the dresses he had approved of and those he did not like. She wanted to look good for him when he had calmed down and returned.

To cut a long story short, he kept on coming back, using the original lines to try to charm her again and she fought hard but now and again gave in until the cycle of love and hurt had turned over and over enough.

Her thoughts ran and ran never finding resolution. She was like her grandfather, trapped in a place where he did not have freedom to walk around and chat to others. Likewise, she was always being told where to go and what to do.

Now, she needed to check her parachute after all. One by one she looked for the strings that held the canopy to the harness. She needed to eject herself from the flaming wreck of her life but the strings of her protection had been cut and removed. No friends, no family apart from her grandmother who would not accept being distanced.

She sat quietly, scratched her head and almost on a whim, spoke into the air asking her grandfather for help.

At that moment, her grandmother phoned. 'Hi, Sophie. It has been a while since I heard from you. I hope all is good with you.'

The sobbing noise spoke instead of words.

'Your grandad told me a lot about people who want to control for their own pleasure. He called them non-return-valves'. His boss was like that. A self-serving lump off what a dog leaves behind. When my lovely man had been pushed enough, he jumped and pulled the cord but the strings had been cut. There were stories spread that his land-scaping ideas were too idiotic, too expensive and customers had complained. Well, this was even before he had started his new business. So, he was a wise man and not only did he wear a parachute but he also had a reserve. When the first one did not work because it had been sabotaged, he used his emergency chute to float down onto solid ground and then he began his new career that took off almost immediately.

'I am not too sure why I wanted to tell you that bit of his life, our lives really, but it was almost as if grandad whispered in my ear and asked me to tell you that you must open your reserve-chute, please. If he, Jeremy or whatever his name is, crashes and burns it is not your fault. He just enjoyed being a self-centred fool who used your kind heart to build himself up.'

After they had hung up, Sophie blocked Jeremy's number from her phone, blocked him on social media, deleted photographs and began to feel the tug of the first string on her chute.

Then she started phoning her family and friends, explaining that she had been through a difficult time and said she wanted to reinstate contact. What she got back was sympathy and understanding. She learnt that she was not the only person to be caught by an emotional predator.

All the strings restored on her parachute and her reserve one repacked, she drove to visit her grandfather's grave with a big bunch of red roses. She chatted about what had happened and thanked him for his good advice.

On her return home, she stopped at the flower shop and bought another bunch of roses which she gave to her grandmother.

Little was said that was not spoken in hugs and smiles.

The parting words Sophie heard were simple. 'Grandad doesn't need a parachute where he is, Angels have their own wings.'

They both winked, smiled, looked to the skies and said, thank you.'

THE GHOST RETURNS

A long time after her experience with Kevin, Dianna pondered long and hard about the events that had changed her as a person during those years.

She considered the strategy of having lots of attention in the beginning and then the withdrawal and no contact that followed. For her, the term ghosting meant very little. She did not believe in ghosts and she saw no reason why they would appear and just as suddenly disappear.

She thought of it more as being an animal being trapped in a cage. In the beginning there would be abundant food and nourishment. Then the meals would be withdrawn and the poor creature would have to wait for the master to return to throw sustenance back into the coop.

Perhaps it was because she had not given enough love and affection. Perhaps her lover had another pet or pets that he needed to see to get the warmth that she had been unable to provide.

She blamed herself for her loss. After all, he had been a really nice man at the beginning. They shared common interests and he paid her so many compliments that she had been overwhelmed. Then, through her stupidity, she thought, she had let him slip out of her hand and into others grasping for the love they knew they would get from him.

She missed him every time he went away and was desperate to speak to him in order to tell him her feelings, and to apologise for being so unworthy. It was always to no avail. He did not answer her calls because he had blocked her and it was devastating to her that he would not get them when she was alone and isolated from him.

She would cry and cry. She would stop eating in case he thought she was overweight. She would wear makeup and smart clothes for when, and if, he made a surprise return to her.

She had enjoyed being controlled by Kevin. He chose her clothes, her appearance generally and so she knew that when she did as she was told, then he would be grateful for her efforts. Yet, whatever she did, even at his command, was never good enough for him. She concluded that she was useless and a failure at pleasing the man she loved.

Purely by chance, one evening she turned on the TV and she looked for films. One she found was about a nun who felt trapped and unfulfilled in a nunnery where she found no reward in praying and wanted to satisfy more earthly desires. She wanted warm love from a human rather than the colder love she had to encounter in the cloisters. The nun, a beautiful woman hidden beneath a dark habit, stripped off her uniform of faith to the spirits she could not see, took clothes that had been given to be sold to provide funds for the convent and walked out.

She walked to her brother's house, knocked on the door and was welcomed. As a nun, she had been a lost sister in both senses of the word and her brother and sister-in-law provided clothes and funds for her. They even sent a cheque to the convent to pay for the clothes Sister Mary had taken.

It all ended happily when Mary met and fell in love with one of her brother's friends.

'It only happens in the movies', Dianna said as she sobbed. Something must have been triggered in her mind. The next day, she went out to a clothes shop and bought what she wanted to wear. She changed her underwear and shoes. She bought makeup and perfumes she liked and went home with her arms being stretched by the weight of her bags. Once in the house, she ripped off her blouse and skirt she had been told to buy to suit Kevin's taste, and put them in a plastic sack. She took off her disliked sexy bra and pants and threw them in the bin along with her old

70

makeup.

She got into a warm bath and scrubbed herself. She shampooed her brown locks and laughed as she sang, 'I'm Going to Wash That Man Right Out of My Hair', dried herself and dressed in her new clothes.

She thought she would phone some of her long-neglected friends.

They were wonderful. They had heard about how narcissists would ghost their victims in order to weaken them while. they were actually getting it off with other women. They congratulated her on breaking away at last. They had been aware that Dianna had been distant

That evening, she decided that she would watch another film.

The doorbell rang and she opened it. Kevin tried to march in but she blocked him.

'So, the ghost has returned to haunt me again.' For Dianna, ghosting was about a deliberate withdrawal to allow feelings for him to grow while he was getting his feed from another victim. Having seen through him, it was not difficult to rid her life of her cause of misery.

Kevin ignored what she had said and shouted, 'You look different. What the hell have you done to yourself.' He was angry and his face glowed red.

Dianna replied. 'I am different. I am not your faithful dog that puts up with the occasional whipping, nor am I going to live with an unfaithful and evil man who just wants to have his women living in his zoo.

'We are done, go away and never come back here again.' She was better than him because she avoided threatening what might happen if he did.

Luckily a neighbour had just pulled up and sat in his car watching. He tooted his horn and waved so that Dianna and Kevin both knew he was there watching and protecting.

Kevin, while still standing on the doorstep, tried to lie his way out of the situation. He explained that he needed to get away to see his sick mother before she died and he did not want to disturb her by receiving calls.

He had forgotten that he had already told Dianna that his mother had died years ago to gain her sympathy and care.

Dianna wanted no arguments. She told Kevin very firmly to go back to where he had been. She guessed that he was getting his need for a supply of love from elsewhere and she was done.

She was a smart thinker and she knew that it is almost certain that when the parting happens, she would be the subject of an avalanche of insults, name calling and accusations because the mirror he had tried to create in her would reflect back what he really thought about himself.

She told him to go away from her life for ever and pushed the door to close it.

As she had predicted, he swore, accused her of infidelity and various other slurs before she shut the door firmly, put the security chain in its slot and, through the window, observed him speed away. Her neighbour watched him go and his role as body guard came to an end. His wife and children came out to welcome him home.

The following day, Dianna decided to go to the charity shop with her old clothes that Kevin had forced her to buy after she had washed and dried them. She remembered that they might be a source of a change of role and life for a real Sister Mary in the neighbourhood.

Dianna was embarrassed by the volume of her laughter when she was choosing her evening movie. 'Ghostbusters would be a great choice', she thought.

REFLECTING ON RELATIONSHIPS

At the beginning when the mirror was bought, it was placed in the bedroom where it would admire Charles.

As time went by, without understanding why because Charles had no empathy, not even for his reflection in the mirror. He spoke to himself and made demands that the shadow that looked back at him gave him praise but it was always silent. It had no words of its own, it could only repeat what Charles said. He could not understand why the image he saw and admired could not return those feelings back to him.

No matter how hard he smacked the glass in temper, or how much he polished it as a sign of his love for it, nothing happened. There was no magic in their relationship, no love, no respect and no trust. Charles was convinced that his mirror chatted away behind his back and that it talked to other people's reflections when they were alone. It was an unfaithful cheat and needed to be isolated as a punishment.

In his life away from the cause of his misery, he did not understand why people seemed to want to fix him. He knew that he could not feel what other people felt but there again, he did not care. As long as they had the ability to love and adore him, he felt satisfied to an extent but never fully happy because they were unable to give him the maximum dose that he demanded.

In fact, he knew that it was something wrong in them, and he blamed others for never getting the point. He openly criticised them for never delivering the piles of compliments and praise he had given at the beginning but which he curtailed because they were too stupid to give it back.

He would walk away so that they could learn what to do but most of the women he met were slow learners and so he had to train them like dogs. A bit of praise and a lot of pain for not learning how to perform.

They were all like the bloody mirror in his room. No matter what he gave, they were unable to give anything back. They were bloodsuckers who wanted more and more. They wanted him to listen to their chattering, they wanted to go out on their own. They wanted to contact friends and family without realising how much anguish that caused him. He was not a jealous person like they were. He was only concerned with their welfare in a dangerous world where other men wanted to take advantage. They were so much better off being alone with just him to be their soulmate.

Sure, he had other girlfriends who needed looking after and he made himself available to keep them company and only required them to compliment him and to show devotion.

They were all so different to the mirror in many ways but everything was selfish. They could not understand why the relationships always seemed strained and would eventually break up.

As he reflected upon the women in his life, he punched the mirror to punish all of them.

'Nobody understands me, not even you.' The shards of glass fell to the floor and stayed there. It was easier to walk away and move into a different room than to recognise the mess he had made.

'I don't need an inanimate object to tell me how wonderful I am when there are real human beings out there who are willing to tell me.'

THE MAZE

Mazes are fascinating things. Made by humans, they have so many elements of mystery, love and fear.

In building them, knowledge is power. Setting up a maze and knowing how to get in and out are controls over others when they are made to feel lost. It is a metaphor for finding love and becoming abandoned.

Whatever tempts a person in must contain a sense of enticement and intrigue. The leaves on the hedges give protection but when people are lost, they become entrapment.

Stephanie was in love with Matt and she thought he was in love with her. As in the movies, she declared that she would do anything for him, no matter what he asked.

It was a warm morning when they went to visit the maze. As if intended as a special day, there were no other people there. It belonged to the happy couple.

Matt was charming and caring. He told her that there would be a special surprise when they got to the centre, the core of the vast expanse of hedges that made paths into the unknown territory.

Matt stood at the entrance, blew a kiss, and beckoned for Stephanie to follow him.

Like a young girl on her first date, she jogged her thirty-two-year-old body along

to catch up with her beau.

She hardly noticed the small bushes that made the hedges. Their verdant green leaves passed her by as she slowed to a walk and searched for Matt. He had disappeared quickly and had left her to make her own way. As she decided to take a right turn rather than go straight on or left, he appeared. He had a big grin on his face.

'You must do what I tell you or you will get lost. I am your guide, your best friend and I will look after you.'

She could have turned to find her way back to the entrance, but she carried on. She trusted Matt. And to be honest, she was looking forward to getting to the middle where she would pull off her clothes and they would make beautiful, wonderful and private love hidden from the world.

That was the excitement she wanted and that she never got from her previous boyfriends or her ex-husband. She was a free agent and wanted to live life to the max.

She continued the game. It was as if it was blind man's bluff. He was out of sight but would suddenly jump out, praise her and then wait for her to outbid him in compliments and praise. If she failed to meet his needs, he would go away again and leave her blaming herself for her loss.

It was a cloudy day so she was unable to use the sun to navigate her way. Every turn she made seemed to get her deeper and deeper into the puzzle. And every step she took made the leaves seem darker as the bushes were taller and thicker. There were moments of panic. She called out to Matt for help but he would only find her on his terms. He needed more and more praise, more and more attention and then, as if to taunt her, he would tell her he needed a bigger incentive if she wanted his help.

So, she was alone, lost and fearful. She knew she could not find either the middle or the exit on her own. She was reliant on him and his ability to steer her on the correct route.

His voice kept appearing from nowhere telling her she must be crazy and mad, at not being able to find her way. She was so stupid that she could not even follow simple instructions.

The ground was hard, the grass had withered away from the lack of sunlight and she had nobody in this place apart from him. She was isolated and abandoned but she knew Matt held her lifeline.

She wondered how Matt was so adept at finding where she was and in which direction she should journey. It occurred to her that she was not the first woman he had taken to the maze. He knew what was what and how to go about things.

There were small spaces where she could relax a little where the light penetrated the dense foliage but she was soon waved on to find the target. As before, the further in she got, the hedge got bigger and thicker obscuring most of the light and her view.

She would find another small clearing where she felt scared. There were sounds of wild and menacing creatures and the hiss of snakes which she quiickly moved away from to go further and further in. To encourage her, he would appear, threaten and then disappear again leaving her feeling lost and desperate for his return. And it seemed that the more she accepted demands the higher the hedges grew for some reason that she was unable to comprehend.

She started to come to her conclusion that what Matt wanted was control rather than sharing. He demanded her love and devotion but gave nothing in return apart from insecurity and her desperate attempts to regain those first moments of him being a kind, caring and gentle spirit of happiness.

She decided that she would remove him from her life and even though imprisoned, she rebelled and pushed him away. He roared in anger but then, as if by magic, the hedges got lower. She saw the goal, the place where he had promised her the world. Rather than being paradise, it was a dry and barren patch with an empty cup placed onf the table. She picked it up and laughed. Rather than drinking from a chalice overflowing with joy and fulfilment, it was a beaker with dirty water in it.

She spoke to herself. 'This is nothing more than a beaker full of empty promises made by a man who is a manipulative blood sucker. I have no need of you to find my way out, my eyes are now wide open and I can see everything perfectly.' She tipped the water away and as she did so, the hedges seemed to start losing their leaves. She could see the road she had taken and how to get out easily.

The sun started to shine as she heard a loud cursing in the distance. 'When I catch you, you will pay just like the others did. You have ruined my life by being the selfish bitch I thought you were. I will make you pay. You never loved me like I loved you.'

Stephanie closed her ears to the noise and walked to the entrance which was now her exit from the most horrific journey she had ever undertaken.

His final words confirmed everything she had realised in that flash of insight.

'I will come back with a woman who is able to see what a wonderful man I am. Somebody who will do my bidding and be grateful.'

As she expected, and had been told, a few months after the trip to the maze, Matt phoned her and asked if she was alright and how much he missed her. He invited her for a drink in a neutral place so that they could chat. She put the phone down and let him carry on without listening. When the line went dead, she blocked his number and poured herself a drink to celebrate her uncontrolled and free life.

One day, she was reading about mazes to discover why Matt had taken her, and others, into one. Then she stumbled upon the Greek myth about the Minotaur who devoured people. 'That seems to fit him. The consumer of emotions.'

When she then looked at the words about the monster in the labyrinth, she burst out laughing. The Minotaur was half man and half bull.

'That would be right. He was only half a man when he was in

bed and the other half was bullshit.'

Her new boyfriend, Robert, gave her a cuddle and asked why she was laughing. She explained. He knew all about Matt and he, rather being jealous of another man in her life, was totally supportive, kind and loving.

Stephanie was happy at being with a man who demanded nothing but was happy to give with no expectation of her giving anything back, although she did because they were on a balanced level of trust and understanding. He never had a maze to trap and blackmail women into begging for help.

HOT AIR

It was a strange thing standing in a field just after sunrise. Sarah walked towards the monumental head of Jimmy who was smiling at her. She laughed and was full of joy in the moments just before she heard the pop of a champagne cork as she climbed into the basket.

'Welcome aboard Sarah. Are you ready for the best day of your life?'

Her reply was loud, 'Of course I am. I want to spend my life with you as well as this one day.'

They hugged and as she was telling him how much she loved him, he untied the ropes that were holding the balloon on the ground. It seemed that the more she told him how warm and loving she felt, the higher they got.

Floating on the wind, they were happy as they drank and munched away on Belgian chocolates. Jimmy was a hero. Romantic and delightful as they drifted along.

He seemed to be bored when she talked about how pretty the land was below them but perked up when she talked about him in glowing terms.

The balloon started to descent slowly and Jimmy asked for more compliments and praise. Sarah obliged and the big envelope rose higher.

Jimmy was in charge, he was the pilot and he showed off his skills as best he could. Unable to navigate, he pretended that he was flying on a course of his choice. He assumed, incorrectly, that Sarah would have no idea about how the craft sailed on the breeze.

He needed more praise to keep to the altitude he wanted and he shouted at her when it slowed down. She was beginning to realise that she was being used and after she had told him that she wanted some praise in return, he threatened to throw her out of the basket. That made her scared and when the rain started, she was not sure if it was her or the coldness of the storm that made the balloon start to drop.

'More compliments, I need more praise and devotion or else. Unless you praise my looks, my skills, my ability to make you happy, then you will have to go before we crash.'

His words made her colder towards him and the balloon started to deflate. As they rushed to the ground, he swore, he cursed, he threatened even more.

'What should have been a wonderful trip has been ruined by you. You have spoiled everything, you ungrateful bitch.'

The little airship landed with a bump and bounced around until it stopped.

He told her to get out and pushed her to the ground as she was doing so. 'I only wanted you as ballast but you have served your purpose now.

She watched as the handsome face that had been on the canopy changed. She saw Jimmy's angry face looking at her, the smile had gone.

She ran away as fast as she could before he could hurt her with his evil words of abuse. She tripped and as she laid on the grass, she heard the sound of a champagne cork popping as Jimmy said, 'Welcome aboard Miranda. Are you ready for the best day of your life?'

The reply was loud, 'Of course I am. I want to spend my life with you as well as this one day.'

The balloon rose into the sky as Sarah puked and cried with sadness at first and then, with relief.

THE NATURE OF NATURE

When we look at nature for inspiration in storytelling, it is easy to talk about hunters and gatherers. The drive to gather food is for the survival of the individual and the propagation of the species.

Mankind is the only species that hunts and gathers for pleasure. It seems to symbolise a feeling of superiority. Where the alpha males and females appreciate the chase and the search for trophies rather than for sustenance. Success becomes a badge of honour which has to be admired and praised by the community. Heroes are made and their prowess is what drives them.

Nonsense, I feel some readers are muttering. What about things like the female praying mantis that after mating, consumes her mate. That is not for the delight of victory, it is part of the system that ensures that the mother-to-be has a supply of nourishment for the forthcoming offspring that carry their father's genes into the next generation. That is about survival instead of enjoyment.

It is a similar tale when spiders are involved. Although, like humans, they set traps that catch their prey, poison their catch, wrap it up and then consume what they have caught for nutrition, not for their reputations as the best. Some humans, male and female are skilled at setting traps that will catch their emotional prey. Usually in a web of lies rather than sticky threads. The predator waits, watches, studies and plans its attack and when to seize.

Moving along, a honey bee is dangerous when provoked but is a delight to watch when it is feeding on nectar that will become honey. That honey attracts humans who will take it even though that can be hazardous unless done safely with smoke and netting.

The bees never make honey to attract people so that they can sting them. They only do that to protect their supply of food that the nurse bees will need to give to the larva to grow and in turn, become collectors of nectar or guards to protect the hive.

It gets more deadly when nectar is used like the gentle and loving words of a narcissist to attract and obtain its next source of feed. The Venus Fly Trap is just one of a big collection of carnivorous plants that offer sweetness to the insects that want to consume easily acquired treats. Strangely, after the fly or whatever enters the trap, it can consume happily until it touches the triggers within a short space of time. Then the plant closes and excretes its digestive juices to drain the life and fluids from the victim. Sounds familiar, Huh?

We can finish this story off by directing at human hunters of anything from something as large as an elephant to something as small as a butterfly. As far as can be aware, neither of the ends of that range are consumed as sources of nutrition. They are killed because it pleases the catcher.

And a comparison can be made with leisure fishermen who catch and release. They get their thrills but they also act in a humane way unless they are angling for fish to eat, which is acceptable.

The butterfly collector is a bit of an oddity. He or she catches beauty for the simple reason that they want to kill it, mount it on a board and then look at its glory. Is it not better to let the butterflies flutter around, breed and create more of the colourful creatures. They marvel at the beauty of the deceased beings that fill our skies with different shapes and shades of splendour as they chase around looking for mates.

There is a something in nature that is worth mentioning. Moles and shrews keep captive live prey. Shrews deliver venom that paralyses their live captives so that they have a supply of food. Moles have toxins in their saliva that will immobilise earthworms which are deposited in chambers specially dug for the purpose of storage.

Here we get the similarity of words with narcissists and the other apparently cuddly mammals. Toxic, captive and paralysis or the lack of the ability to escape. Sounds all too familiar. However, those little critters save food in larders to survive when times get bad. When the ground is covered in snow and when their sources of food are well hidden or hibernating. It is a simple case of put food into storage or stave.

For the human predators of emotion, it is different. They want their supplies for sure, but they depend on the capture of souls who will feed them with the love, affection and praise they demand. Without that they never starve to death, they just feel sorry for themselves because they, being perfect in their own imaginations, can never understand the rejection if one or more of their reserves fails to deliver by breaking contact, regaining their own sense of self-worth that has been prised away from them. So the shrews and moles have to do what they do to provide for themselves. The narcissists do what they do to bolster their own egos and sense of being perfect and wonderful.

To make the metaphor more complete, love bombing is the same as the first dose of toxic input. The purpose is to stun the prey, to stop escape. If they do their best to run away then they will have other doses of charm, flattery and promises of undying love. They become trapped in the emotional cages that will make them return what is expected to avoid being hurt. The hypnotic toxins can change minds, create dependency and the fear of being lonely and unloved.

Do you want to know a secret? The toxins are weak and their effect broken with the antidote of pride in recognising what is happening and then, as if by magic, the cage opens and you can break out.

Why is it that we humans are the only living things that enjoy inflicting emotional pain and torture on others. Sure, there is a circle of life that involves being born, growing up, mating, producing young that we care for and love because we have humanity. When that last word is missing then we become pleasure seekers by hurting others with psychological and physical pain.

Maybe because our ancestors allegedly found women, knocked them out with clubs and then dragged them back to their caves for sex and enslavement, we still have that that primitive drive in some of our fellows.

The rest of us become either victims or become like the guard bees keeping raiders from the hive of innocence.

SCULPTORS OF PERFECTION

Let's imagine cartoon like thought bubbles over their heads.

'Shall I compare thee to a summer's day?

'My goodness, you are good looking'. (Nearly as attractive as I am.)

'You are as if sunlight has suddenly come into my life' (to brighten my sense self-love.)

'Before you, there was nothing' (apart from a load of other victims)

'I want to be your sculptor who takes something ordinary like mud, and moulds it into something of such beauty that will nearly match my own but, alas will never equal it.

'To prove my point, I will lower your self-esteem. I will tell you that although your cooking is sort of alright, it is never as good as what I have experienced before.

'To save words, substitute the words 'sex' and 'looks' for cooking.

'When I first met you, I told you that you were beautiful. Then it changed to pretty and then you became 'fairly attractive'.

'I like to chip away at what made you in the first place. I am a sculptor, I told you.

'I will carve away your friends and family. You need to concentrate on the artist, me, who is modelling you.

'I will make decisions on your body shape and features to suit what I want and to get rid of what you admire about yourself.

'Bigger or smaller boobs, a rounder or flatter stomach, a bouncy backside or perhaps one that needs slimming.

'When you become my mannequin, then I will have to choose clothes for you. They will have to be very sexy and show off your figure, but yet there again, you will not be able to wear them in places where others can see your body that I have made perfect. I did that for me, sorry, I mean us to express how much you mean to me and you must tell me how grateful you are to be made into a statue that would look good in an art museum. But there again, it would be too public. You will remain here where I can see you. You are so valuable that I will have to be your security guard preventing others from seeing and probably stealing you.

'Shall I compare thee to a summer's day? Or perhaps to me?''

The only comparison to be made is the one summer day which is wrecked by a big storm that drenches everything and drowns any love that was there at the beginning.

SNAKE CHARMERS AND LION TAMERS

Some people admire snake charmers for the risk they take. With a pipe playing, they stare a cobra in the face as it sways from side to side. Just a quick strike and the charmer would be killed. Such bravery, such a lot of admiration and respect for the man who is risking everything.

The snake has been hypnotised by the movement of the punji as music is played on that instrument. In truth, it has not been mesmerized at all.

To be honest, the snake is defenceless. Having been caught, it has probably had its fangs removed after swinging it around by its tail to remove venom by centrifugal force. Then the fangs are snapped off or pulled out with pliers.

Sometimes the mouths are stitched closed and the snakes will die after a while from starvation and dehydration.

Now powerless, it is unable to hunt for food or to meet others of its kind. It is kept prisoner in a basket and fed and watered very little. It now relies on the charmer for its existence even though it sees the man and the pipe as its enemy.

The 'dancing' or swaying is a defensive response to what it perceives as an attack by the man and the pipe.

All in all, the snake is the victim and the charmer is not really charming. The serpent has been made the property of the man who controls it and decides on how it will be treated. The main focus the charmer has is to avoid being hurt and this means that his victim is the one who suffers from neglect and being forced to do what is expected.

And there will be other snakes after one has served its purpose and it when it dies, its skin is sold.

Enter the narcissist. He or she has a similar story. The victim is caught and then treated in such a way that the defences are broken down so that an attack in self-defence is less likely to have any effect.

Freedom is restricted and contact with like spirited people is closed down. The victim is in the metaphorical basket making their appearances at the summoning of the 'charmer'.

Like the snake charmer, the human charmer needs respect from others for the risks being taken from, what is actually harmless having been muted and overpowered. The snake has no fond feelings for the person who has captured and maltreated it apart from an intense loathing which might be reduced when it is given a drink of water, or for the human charmer, a kind word and a reduction of verbal and sometimes physical abuse.

The snake man will always know where to get more to replace those he has in baskets as will the human enchanter who needs his supply of respect and admiration. There is a difference here between the two. The man with the serpent gets his admiration from the crowd who also give money to reward his bravery. He is made to feel special and they beguile people with their skill at controlling something so dangerous.

Yet there are plenty in the crowd who despise the man with the pipe for his cruelty and abuse of a creature that was born to be free. The real predator in the mix is the human who needs something that is beautiful and is feared. The snake charmer creates an illusion and profits from it. The snake receives very little in return because they are there solely to benefit the charmer.

And now, we will move on to a different animal in the same situation. Lions and lionesses are stunning and threatening in the wrong situation. Perfect for the tamer who creates the impression that he or she has power over something which is so much bigger and stronger than they are. Like the snake charmers, the sense of awe and respect comes from the onlookers, the spectators. With memories of slaves being attacked and killed in the Roman amphitheatres, their reputation for being powerful predators is well known.

As before, the idea that a seemingly vulnerable human (who as a narcissist is a different kind of predator) can overcome a mighty beast, earns all sorts of admiration from nearly everybody, apart from the lion. Maybe in the beginning, the lion was well looked after, fed without the risks of hunting and welcomed the new life until the training began.

In earlier times, big cat training was based of beating the animal into submission but in more modern times different methods, based on psychology are used. Now we get close to the narcissist. When the desired behaviour is performed, then a treat is offered. The lion likes that and does it again. However if it fails to do what the tamer wants, then the reward is withheld.

This is classic conditioning so that the operator gets what it wants from the subject it wants to dominate.

There is salvation, lions can be trained but never tamed, it is said. In a narcissistic relationship, it is important to know that. The victim is also strong and fully capable of resisting the attempts at curbing and conditioning to fulfil the needs of the trainer.

Unlike the poor animals in baskets or cages, every human has the ability to break free from domination.

EMOTIONAL PARASITES AND SYMBIOSIS

Without getting too squeamish, parasites are things that take from another for their own benefit and leave the provider weak and often diseased. They influence and manipulate in order to survive. There is always only one motive and that is for the benefit of the pest and it rarely helps the host. It is an easy way of life. Food is provided and energy is taken for living without a single 'thank you' in return. With narcissistic parasites, the assets, physical, material and emotional can be used to please the parasite. They are not pretty things to others but they manage to invade the lives of people in a destructive way.

The other side of the coin involves symbiosis. This is where one organism gains from another for mutual advantage. A strange example is the relationship between sharks and cleaner fish. One is helped by the much smaller fish to remove parasites whilst being protected by the much bigger and more aggressive friendly guard.

Other examples include bees that take nectar in return for carrying pollen to other plants to reproduce.

Both parties involved are happy. When a relationship is based on common desires then it is healthy. When it is based on a one-sided need then it is very bad news.

We do not need to continue with this story. The point has been made in a few simple words.

NARCISSISM, THE MUSICAL

So many stories have hit the stage as musicals. It is worth a try with this one.

It is quite confusing trying to make a decision about the title for this piece.

It could be **All the World's a Stage,** or **Play Acting,** maybe **Building the Best Mousetrap.**

Anyway, I am a reviewer of plays, theatre, entertainment of all sorts. I am not a critic; they were all on the stage.

I went along to watch what was billed as the greatest show of a fictional plot that had many so different layers of performers.

All the actors were playing the parts of people that they were not. It was all pretence. They did their best to warm the audience up, to get them to transform from punters to fans.

As a reviewer, I was confused by the cocktail of the acts. It ranged from drama to circus; Shakespearean tragedy to silent movie slapstick.

I will evaluate each act in the order in which they appeared.

Da, da, da, da. The big crimson drapes drew back to reveal the stage. The gaslights flickered as they reflected from the mirrored backdrop. A steady drumbeat at the pace of a lover's heart quietened the crowd and it started.

The first on was the Master of Ceremonies. 'Roll up, roll up, roll up. Welcome to the greatest show on Earth'.

What on Earth? Harry the heckler had started his unbilled act.

The MC was booed off by the other members of the cast. 'He is no master of anything. I should be doing that.' The combined voices of the actors became the mad ranting of a huge mass of dissidents.

So, after a moment or two, a trio came onto the platform. Two men and a woman called the Three Am-egos. One by one they were introduced. Tom, Dick and Harriet.

They tuned up with the orchestra helping. Dough, Ray and ME, ME, ME, ME, ME……

Tom began with a song he had written himself called, 'Self-Validating', about how wonderful he was at doing everything that he wanted. It had a chorus that he wanted the audience to sing along with about this magnificent person they were looking at with amazement in their eyes. Most, no all, refused.

Next, Dick sang with a deep bass voice, 'Self-Indulgent'. He sang the song to a different tune that was being played because that is what he wanted to do. 'Screw you', he shouted at the conductor.

Then Harriet joined in with her song, 'Self-Centred'. She pushed the other two to one side, told them to go because she was in control. She wanted to please herself rather than entertaining the concertgoers and she sang along to the pre-recorded backing track that was made by overdubbing her own voice numerous times.

They did what they wanted without regard for the onlookers at all. Despite ignoring the needs of the people who had bought tickets, they sneered at them, told them they were an awful crowd and stormed off like a threesome of spoiled brats.

Next, a different singer walked on. The woman sang. It was awful and when she stopped, there was no applause. She then just stood in her place and sulked in silence. She wanted to be acknowledged, to be liked and she refused to budge. The assembly did cheer, however, when a big hook reached out, wrapped around her neck and dragged her off.

She was replaced by yet another singer who was also bad. He

got no response and started shouting at the top of his voice about how ungrateful the ignorant listeners were. At the end of his long rant, he stormed off.

Now all of this would have been entertaining had it been a comedy rather than a farce.

A classical actor, dressed in clothes that suggested the era of Kings and Queens waltzed his way to the footlights and started quoting lines from Shakespeare. 'Yond Cassius hath a lean and hungry look. He thinks too much; such men are dangerous.'

'Hungry for power and control', a heckler shouted.

'Power is not a means; it is an end.' Was the reply. 'George Orwell said that'.

'I wish your act would end', the heckler continued.

The reply was simple, 'As Machiavelli suggested, He who wishes to be obeyed must know how to command.'

'You are so bad.' The heckler wanted the last word.

'Remove the troublemaking idiot.' The actor gave his command to the security guards.

They obeyed him and physically dragged him from the stage.

Then the music for the stripper came on. There were cheers and wolf-whistles from the men as they stood up in their seats for a better view as the big busty blond wiggled her way onto the middle of the arena. 'Hello everyone. I am Pearl Eske'. Her sultry tones were like a love tonic being gargled.

Her body was hidden by big feathers that she used to tantalise and to make the hormones flow.

As she danced slowly and evocatively, she dropped the concealment from the plumage and reached behind her back. She unclipped and pulled her empathy into full view. She whirled it around and threw it into the crowd. Men and women scrambled

97

to collect it.

Next was care which she did not seem to care for as she slipped it off and stood on it. She had just a few bits left on, her 'isms'. Altruism, humanitarianism and purism. She was standing nearly naked and she teased again with her feathers. She flashed her narcissism and egotism before telling the viewers to get a life as she marched away with an obscene gesture.

One member of the cast who was difficult to measure was Gordon the Ghost. He would appear, shout out accusations and then walk off. Then much later he would walk on, listen to applause and then stay for a while before throwing out threats and then disappear again. He did this too many times and he just created frustration and eventually dislike.

One man, Mr Wonderful, professed to be a mind reader who would say what others were thinking. He was easy to figure out. Most of what his helpers thought was, actually, what he had planted in their heads already by using fairly coercive methods.

If I may say so, Frank the ventriloquist was crap. The dummy was a life-sized model of himself who would repeat what his operator said and vice versa. It was so bad that the dummy's mouth would move while it was talking to Frank and when Frank was talking to the dummy, his lips would wobble. They obviously enjoyed each other's company and they were the only real friends that either of them had, but they were a tedious part of the show.

I could carry on with the others but enough is enough. We had Sharp Tongue, the knife thrower who threatened the women volunteers who were pinned to his target.

Then, acrobats would leave people dangling not knowing what

to do for their own health and safety.

I think that was when I fell asleep. I could not stand watching and listening to any more.

The finale woke me up. The whole cast appeared when the curtain was opened again. They stood in a row in front of the huge mirror that made the backdrop. The folk in the seats closest to the stage noticed that all of the performers had their backs to the audience. They were wearing handsome and pretty masks that created the illusion that they were all normal human beings. If you could see the real faces that were drawn into angry scowls and grimaces, the truth about how they interacted could be seen. They all hated each other because each single performer wanted to be considered the best.

They all looked at the entertainer they liked the most. That was the person in the reflection from the mirror in front of them.

The bowed to their images, and as they did so, they pointed their arses towards the people who had wasted their time coming to witness the absurdity of what happened in a life of disorder and misunderstanding.

FINAL WORDS. BEWARE. There is almost certainly a performance of this show in a town near you. It runs all year long but with different actors playing the same parts that have been described.

Thank you for.

RELEVANT STORIES FROM MY OTHER BOOKS

These stories have been published before as part of the author's Omnibus of Short Stories and have been added here as they are applicable to the victims of narcissism.

QUICKSAND

Life can present precarious options. The way to be safe is to avoid the pitfalls that can be offered as pleasures such as bad relationships, drugs or jobs without prospects. Be confident enough to make the right decisions. Take those chances that offer benefit and steer clear of those that offer jeopardy.

The woman was stuck in quicksand in the middle of a forest. The more she struggled to get out, the more she sank. This bog was different to the usual mix of sand and water, it was made from swampy emotion, dank and rank.

She fell into the quagmire when she split from her boyfriend. He had used and abused her for years and when she finally had enough, she became brave for a moment and told him.

He told her she was ugly, fat and useless in bed. He had told her that so many times before and she started to believe that it was true.

And then, after smacking her, he left her to live with somebody else that he could exploit, use and abuse.

She sank into gloom. She immersed herself in thoughts of regret. She had no future and was half happy that she was stuck and half miserable that her life could not progress.

A giant was walking along the same path and he saw the woman in the quicksand. He was unable to get close enough to save her because he was so heavy that he would sink in himself.

He stood back and unravelled a rope from his backpack. He threw it to the woman who grabbed it.

The giant pulled and pulled and pulled until the woman was freed and was able to stand on solid ground.

She was grateful and thanked the giant.

'Who are you?' She asked.

The giant replied with a voice as deep as thunder. 'I am your future. When somebody is stuck, they have to be aware that the future is what pulls them out of the sticky situation that they are in. Now that you are on the outside of the mire, you are standing on higher ground and you can look for safer paths to walk than the one you were on. When you are stuck in a deep quicksand you can only see the mess that you are in. When you stand tall you can see the options that you have in your life. Your boyfriend was the bait that enticed you into the mud. Now you are free from him, rejoice. He will be the quicksand for other souls that I will have to rescue.'

With that speech over, the giant very carefully walked to a big tree at the edge of the forest and tied the rope around its trunk. He then threw the rope back to the woman.

'Use this rope to make to your journey safe. At the end of this rope is where your future starts. Look into the open space beyond the forest, visualise your happy future and let it unfold for you.'

The woman replied, 'But I have no future. I am ugly, fat and not good in bed. My ex-boyfriend told me so.'

The giant looked into her eyes as if seeing her soul. 'You are none of those things. Some men feel that they can only keep the beautiful things they have by hiding them in a cage of insults. Be as free of that cage as you are of the quicksand. The things he said are not true. He was projecting his own insecurities onto you. Get on with your life. Enjoy it. You have everything that you need to succeed now that you are free.'

The giant moved on and disappeared from view.

The woman wiped the mess from her clothes and started to hold her head high. She could see the many directions in which she could travel onwards, some safe, some dangerous. She followed the rope to the tree. She stood and looked at the meadows in front of her, smiled and started walking.

She now knew that the best way to avoid traps was to foresee the dangers at the start of a journey rather than to get fixed in a dangerous situation.

The giant might not appear the next time!

GRAINS OF SAND

The message is always the same, however. What starts as something caring, loving and supportive can become hurtful and then destructive if violence, either verbal or physical is added.

Soft words of love, gentle remarks and compliments are easy to find and use. They are as usual as grains of sand in the desert. Grains of sand are made by rocks banging into each other. It is erosion; it is the grinding down of boulders over years.

Sand is soft; it is comfortable as are the caresses of the language of adoration and as are the soft embraces of those that we love. Yet it takes only one large pebble to wreck the mind and emotions of the person that we love if it hits them.

Those pebbles can be words, gestures or physical acts. They can be the things that never turn into sand as they strike; they damage the target and consequently bounce back to hurt the thrower.

And how many ways can this story be told?

Snowflakes, snowballs and avalanches.

Soft rain drops, water cannons and floods.

Gentle breezes, gales and tornadoes.

The message is always the same, however. What starts as something caring, loving and supportive can become hurtful and then destructive if violence, either verbal or physical is added.

What has been damaged can be repaired but never returned to the original state. A grain of sand, a snowflake, a drop of water a puff of air will always remind the hurt person of the pain that was the outcome in other times.

THE BLACK TUNNEL

Without looking forward people stumble and fall and never find the way out. Whenever a person is in a dark tunnel there is light and cheer if they look for it.

The person walked forward through the tunnel. It was dark, it was cold but it was the only way to go. Yet the end of the tunnel was solid. There would be nothing there apart from the wall that closed off all hope of freedom. This was the life the person lived; trapped in a passage of time that had no exit. Gloom became darker and gloomier as the person walked, nay stumbled, on.

Cries of anguish and pain echoed off the walls, sometimes seeming to mock, sometimes adding to the noise as if the sorrow was being amplified in a huge concert hall. But that, at least, would give space. The tunnel gave noise to its inside and stopped the chaos being heard by the outside world. This was a prison. This was a treadmill of hurt. No way through the floor or the roof. The solidity of this thing that was life, or a miserable symbol of it, the mass, the length of it all worked together to make a depressing and miserable place to be.

"Excuse me. Yes, excuse me." The voice, perhaps an audible hallucination called into the darkness. "Open your eyes and look to the right."

The person had closed both eyes to shut out the darkness of the place even though it was totally pointless to do so.

With eyes open the person looked to the right and saw fields, friends, sunshine and the future.

"What some people are unable to see is that the tunnel is not a tunnel. It is a pathway to a place where the wall opens to show a bright and pleasant future. It is where they meet other people, usually by chance; it is where the sound of laughter drowns out the misery. However, it is necessary to open your eyes to see what is there. Without looking forward people stumble and fall and never find the way out. Whenever a person is in a dark tunnel there is light and cheer if they look for it."

THE BLACK PIT

Depression often goes with being stuck in the poor circumstances that arise when hope evaporates. The important thing to do is to look into the future. See yourself in a better situation; imagine new people in your life. The old saying goes 'be careful what you wish for.' When you live in gloom the light never goes on because you expect the darkness. Do something positive. Turn the light on and bathe in the radiance of optimism. Wish for a happy future. Those bad feelings pass. Depression is a state of mind. We can change that state when we wish for a better future. That has to be our dream that then becomes a reality.

In the darkest despair of depression, the man had the same feeling as if he had fallen from the cliff that faced a narrow ravine.

He fell deeper and deeper into the darkness of the pit. He imagined jagged black rocks at the bottom that would rip his body into many pieces. He was comfortable with that because his misery would end, but somewhere in his heart he wanted a better outcome.

He had closed his eyes at first but he wanted to know when his despair would be saved by his body smashing into the big boulders that awaited him. He was falling more slowly than he thought he should be. Even this fate was full of slowness and waiting for something to happen.

He opened his eyes to see the fate that awaited him.

What he saw was the biggest, bounciest trampoline that there has ever been. It was bright and decorated with pictures of flowers, birds and butterflies. He hit it feet first and the speed at which he fell, slowed.

And then stopped.

He was amazed that he was still alive.

109

Then he started to accelerate upwards and onwards. At first it felt slow and then the pace at which he was being delivered increased until he landed gently on the other side of the canyon. He looked around, astonished by what had happened.

It took him a while to come to a realisation of his situation. There in front of him he could see flowers and butterflies that reflected the patterns on the trampoline.

He could see fields of green grass. He could see pathways that took him into this wonderful place that was light and airy. He could see the friends that he would make in the future.

He looked back to the side of the valley from which he had come. He saw the gloom, the waste, the barrenness, the loneliness that he had experienced. It looked like a dark treacherous desert full of malevolent cacti and poisonous snakes. They swayed as if tempting him to return so that they could hurt him even more.

Every one of his bad experiences seemed to be represented by a part of that landscape that was menacing. Sharp rocks, boggy marshes and debris as if delivered from Hell's waste disposal system.

He turned to face the brighter side. It was if he had travelled from one extreme to the other. Here the landscape was full of beautiful things, every part of this place offered happy and joyful experiences yet to come. Here there were people who were full of delight, full of optimism. The scent in the air had changed from that of rot to that of sweet perfume.

He approached one person who looked friendly, but they all did, and asked if his death had brought him to Heaven.

'No. you are not dead, but now you are alive. You are in the place where we should all live. It is the world as it is without the misery of depression. Without the darkness of pessimism and lack of hope and ambition. This is the real world. What happened to you is that you fell onto an allegorical trampoline that propelled you to a brighter future. It made you aware that life has more to offer than despair.

There is an easier way, however. There is a bridge that spans the canyon. It is made from hope and the desire to look at the future successes of yourself rather than living in the gloom of your supposed failures. It crosses the deep and dark chasm without risk. It is called the Bridge of Positive Thinking. It takes you from a dark state of mind to a bright outlook where happiness is the norm rather than a forlorn dream.'

The man lifted his head and started to plan his life. He thought about what he wanted to do that would make him happy.

He turned his back on the gloomy side of existence and started to walk into the bright side of his life. Soon he was joined by people who shared his hopes and dreams for a better future, his new friends.

He changed his thoughts from those of self-pity to those of self-worth.

NOTE. Of course, there is only a metaphorical trampoline at the bottom of a cliff. Never take the risk of jumping, use the bridge to cross the darkness instead.

THE SCAPEGOAT'S STORY

Highlights the pointless need to assign blame to others.

Way back in time the Scapegoats were big and cuddly animals. They had broad backs and thick skins. They had been specially bred to share the problems of people, which they did with a great sense of pleasure.

However, over time they had been burdened with the task of taking the responsibility and blame for any failings that became apparent in any person's life. Every family had one and, very often, different people would use the same one whenever they felt like it.

Then, one day the Great Creator felt angry at the abuse of these noble creatures and decided to give them liberty. It was decided that they would be reassigned to a much happier life and a plan was devised.

Suddenly, a disease spread through the species which, whilst giving outward signs of pain and terror, actually gave great pleasure as they transformed into their new structures.

So what mankind saw as their extinction was, in fact, the moment of freedom when the Scapegoats were re-created as albatrosses where the breezes would support them effortlessly as they explored the joys of life, rather than its misery.

Naturally, most of humankind decided that this epidemic must have been, after all, the Scapegoat's own fault, so they must have deserved their fate. But the need to give others the blame still remained, and those caring people, who had sympathy for the vanished creatures, very naturally became their substitutes. Although there was nothing different about them when they were born, any weakness that was shown enabled them to be crafted and developed much more easily, by the selfish people, than the years of breeding that would have been necessary to develop a new creature like the original Scapegoats.

Things, or people to blame, were felt to be so essential for a happy life. For example, if the hunt was bad, the men had somebody to rebuke. If a woman felt that her marriage was not working, she could chastise her human Scapegoat.

People could invent all sorts of stories about the reasons for their misery, and assign them to one person. After shifting accountability, they would always feel so much better.

However, the replacements for the Scapegoats had not been bred for the job. Their backs were often not broad enough, nor their skins thick enough to be able to carry the load. Unlike the big creatures before them, they would break down and suffer from their inflicted misery without help. The Blamers would assume that their miserable state was their own failing anyway, so they were shown no sympathy.

The Great Creator was disappointed with this state of affairs and pondered long and hard about what the solution should be. It had to different to the 'plague of delight' that had liberated the first Scapegoats.

Specific elements of a society could not be made immune, and it was not possible to relieve the Blamers of their lack of responsibility for their own actions. That was a self-inflicted condition that came from a lack of care and an abundance of selfishness.

So this time, a two-phase plan came into effect. A 'plague of separation' was spread whereby people could only be with others like themselves.

So, male Blamers would get together to complain about how bad their lives had been because of the women in their lives. Female Blamers, of course, would condemn the men. And so on.

But, after the separation of the two types, the human

Scapegoats had nobody to blame them for anything, so they started to feel unwanted.

And so it happened that after a while, when the human Scapegoats had all left to be together, the Blamers had nobody to blame for what was going wrong with their lives so they had to start blaming each other.

But, as the Blamers thought themselves to be perfect, wars broke out. Many people were destroyed and the population declined. Seeing this devastation, they had no option but to take the blame upon themselves for so much chaos in the World, because nobody else would accept it, and they had to blame somebody.

Meanwhile, the human Scapegoats, being innocent of the bloodshed, started to blame the Blamers for the terrible desolation that now pervaded the Earth.

As planned, after a number of years, the balance between self-accountability and the need to blame those who really were at fault, was achieved in both societies. Now all the people were able to come back together.

People had learnt to accept responsibility for their own mistakes and to work for self-improvement. The Blamers learnt to stop blaming others for the mistakes that they had made themselves. And the Scapegoats learnt to reject any disapproval if they were, in fact, free of error.

At last, everybody was able to offer constructive advice if requested, and they all learnt to withhold unnecessary criticism of others.

But, while the albatrosses lived their lives in peace, the humans started to revert to their old ways.

And who can we blame for that?

THE WIND-BLASTED TREE

When the tree started to grow, it felt isolated. As it poked its growing tip into the air, it was disappointed. There it was, at the top of a wind-blasted hill where a bird must have dropped it as a seed.

It knew that it should be growing tall and straight, but the harder it tried to do so, the harder the wind seemed to blow.

Its roots had to dig deep into the soil and rocks to avoid the sapling from being ripped away by the gales. Its leaves had to hold on very tightly to the twigs and branches to avoid being torn off.

It felt that it was ugly because it was not perfectly shaped like the trees it could see in the river valley below. They were tall, balanced and lush. Birds used their branches to roost and nest. It seemed so very unfair that it was bent and crooked as it grew bigger. And this sense of failure made it stoop even more.

The tree wanted to be admired for its beauty, but it did not feel that beauty was ever attainable. It wanted to be appreciated for its height, but it knew that it would be stunted. Tall branches would be exposed and would be snapped off by the stronger winds.

It wanted to be useful for the birds by offering its branches to hold nests, but it was aware that building materials would be swept away before a nest could be finished.

But what it did not know was that animals, birds and the other plants admired this tree. They could see it from miles away and it became a landmark to help the birds to locate their nests and the land animals to get back to their lairs and dens. Even sailors used it as part of their compass to locate fishing grounds in the sea.

The tree was used in stories to explain the benefits of being tenacious despite adverse conditions.

It would always be explained to young ones in the same way. For example:

"If that tree can grow in such an exposed place, then think what you can do with a much better environment. See how it has adapted to cope with the wind, bending to go with the strength of the gusts rather than fighting back against a stronger force and suffering. Be like that tree. Use your ability to adjust to your surroundings in order to win."

Of course, the tree never heard such praise, and its parents were elsewhere, and unknown, so they could not encourage it to be proud.

One summer's day, the tree was aware of some people sitting in the shade of its branches, leaning their backs against its trunk. They were drawing and painting the view from the top of the hill, but not the tree. The tree felt that it was being used in order to allow the artists to capture the beauty of the landscape whilst at the same time turning their backs on the tree's ugliness. It felt sad. The artists were aware that there was a fine mist was in the air. They thought that it was the start of a sea haze, but it was a fine cloud of tears coming from the leaves.

The artists stopped their work and unwrapped some food. They walked around whilst eating and began to look closely at the tree. They discussed it, they admired it, they praised it so much. They talked about perseverance, determination and fortitude. They talked about it being a monument that was known for miles around. They said that the tree was the main reason for them climbing to the top of the hill.

Then, the tree felt so proud. It was a strange thing, but from that day onwards, the people, birds, animals and the other plants all seemed to notice that the tree appeared to be standing taller and straighter.

BULLY NO MATE'S STORY
From Womb to Tomb
by Jack Mason

This is an account of real-life abuse by a narcissist, love bomber, coercive controller, a horrible and abusive man.

It is told by the brother of the person at the centre of the story, it and reflects real life in many different ways.

BULLY-NO-MATES is a play on words. Billy-no-Mates in the UK, Scot no mates in Australia, Nigel no friends and so on are names for some people who are shunned by others or who choose to reject contact with people who might see what they are doing.

The Eulogy

I have the need to explain what I did and why I am not a bad man for doing it. I needed to sanitise myself and others after the hurt that my sibling caused for so many people throughout his whole life.

What follows is brief. Only good people deserve long stories to be told about them. Billy was so evil that he deserved nothing longer than what I said at his funeral.

It all began by me attempting to write a eulogy for my brother. It was short, and I would like to say, sweet. However, although it was brief, I told the truth, and it was bitter. My words were as follow:

"Billy Mason was a bullying scumbag and narcissist who died with lots of money in the bank but without a single friend in the world. I am only here because I promised that he would be buried after his death."

The undertaker gasped as I walked away to the fresh air outside.

The Womb

I ask myself if it was nature or nurture. For him, I am sure, it was both.

Maybe because his parents had both grown up during the Second World War and his mother had developed an admiration for the armed forces, William and Margaret got together. He was in the navy and his motivation in life was the expression of his masculinity through lust, and for her she wanted to fall in love with a hero. They were opposites but having got her pregnant he did what was expected in those days and married our mother out of obligation. After the reality of marriage sank in, he developed a love for alcohol instead of her. He had been handsome and of good height, mother said, but after the ravages of alcohol and idleness took their toll, I remember him as a man with a strained face and whose crumbling body stumbled around.

My Brother, Billy Mason, was born on the 4th of April 1958 and died sixty-four years later, almost to the day. He was named William, after his father, but was known as Billy-the-Kid by the family to give him his own identity.

A lot of information was given to me by his mother or, in fact, our mother when I was about to become a father for the first time.

She told me that even in the womb Billy was a bully. Yes, he was a little shit even before he was born and remained that way and as he grew he became an even bigger shit. While mother was carrying this monstrous embryo, he was developing his skills at hurting.

Maybe because his father's sperm was damaged by the nuclear tests he witnessed on the Christmas Islands or from the vast amounts of alcohol he drank, something caused his child to be born a horror.

In actual fact, Billy had three fathers. One was the quiet sullen and self pitying one when he had a hangover. The second was the man who enjoyed sitting in the garden come rain or shine, chatting with his imaginary friends while they were apparently sharing copious amounts of scrumpy, a strong cider, and having a whale of a time. The third was the argumentative and violent one who would lash out with evil words, accusations and his fists when he felt he had been taken for a fool, which he was.

Because of the way father was, our family needed money and the local grocer, Mr George, offered mother a job in which she found comfort and a safe haven away from our little council house in a run-down area of a small town in Dorset. That was better than the alternative, a high-rise apartment block in an inner city where the only greenery to see was the mould that grew on the wet and soiled ceiling.

For William, the alcohol caused erectile disfunction and he lost the ability to have sex. I purposefully missed out saying, making love, because he never knew that screwing a woman and making love were two totally different things.

She also told me that when she was carrying Billy, he kicked so hard that it hurt her badly. As if sensing her pain with his embryonic brain, it made him kick again and again, harder and harder as if to signify his ability to cause distress to somebody bigger than himself even though that person was sustaining his life.

Therefore, the question as whether or not his evil controlling and sadistic streak came from nature or nurture is simple. As I said before, I think it came from both.

As father was a jealous man, he accused mother of being a whore. He was even suspicious of people who were out of reach. Apparently, mother had wanted to name me James, after the actor but because James Mason was a handsome man with a smooth voice that was like the purring of a Rolls Royce, William insisted that I should be called Jack, after his father.

During the birth of Billy, mother screamed out loud in agony, distress and hurt. She continued her cries of pain for many years after the delivery of her baby from hell. The hurt was far more severe than the slaps, punches and broken limbs given to her by her husband that would subside over time when he got weaker up until the point when he died in pain, as if karma had taken its revenge.

Growing Up

As I have said, father was a drunk and taught Billy that an argument, a threat and a fist would subdue mother. 'Stand up for yourself, son. Don't let nobody stand in your way.'

The blueprint for the rest of his life was created. He knew what it was like to be hurt for not abiding by his father's rules and practiced his methods on me and our sister Sally. Using threats and punches, he made us do the chores that he had been given so he could watch in comfort during the times father was in his alcohol fuelled world while mother was working in her safe haven of Mr George's grocery shop.

He never praised us for doing well but instead he hit us if we were not perfect, and to his mind, we never were. He enjoyed the power he had over us.

He insisted that mother would buy him smart clothes that would impress others and give the impression that he came from a family that was 'well-off'. He was about the same height and build as his peers but he puffed himself up to pretend that he was bigger. He slicked his dark brown hair down. The Brylcreem boys, the wartime fighter pilots he saw in the films he watched always had good looks and attracted admiration. They also had the added bonus of showing menace when they were in combat.

The only benefit that I got from him was that his hand-me-down shirts, jumpers and trousers were still smart even though showing signs that they were close to being worn out. That ended when I outgrew him. That is when he stopped bullying me.

At school, Billy tried to make his mark and acted the strong man. As a result, the other children called him Silly Billy and after a while he reacted with his fists to stop them. The playground became his battleground.

'I'm not a bully I am Billy. I hate nicknames', he said to the people who behind his back called him Billy the Bully before he found out.

Billy broke toys and if he couldn't keep them he hurt the person to whom they belonged.

That malevolent guidance given to him by father was hard-wired into his mind. He knew from the hot-blooded approach to life that bullying was the best tactic for getting what he wanted. He terrorised other children into pretending that they liked him, or else.

He built a gang around him and he would reward them by not hurting them and by sharing his stolen sweets shoplifted with skill to keep them loyal to his cause which was, of course, himself.

He never had real friends. He thought having people who knew him well was a liability. I know that friends are people you can rely on and they can rely on you. He refused to have any faith in the well-meaning of other people unless he was manipulating them. He saw friends as a weakness. Yet he called people buddies or mates as a method to make them submit to him. He gave a bit of money here and a favour there and they were hooked.

Throughout the rest of his life, self-doubt was his big issue. It was like a monstrous zit that, no matter how hard he squeezed, it just remained and became larger and more fixed on his forehead.

Teenage Years

In the first year of senior school, Billy found that he was the youngest and least grown of the other boys. He realised that a big number of smaller boys had an advantage over a lesser number of the bigger kids. Blood on others was a medal. Blood on himself was a motivation for revenge. They would have to lose much more than he did.

At this new school he needed a different gang and recruited them in the way he did before, sweets, but cigarettes were added to his list. As the boys who were older were full of testosterone from puberty, the best tactic was to show numbers who would potentially be a force rather than going for direct conflict.

He watched the older lads and got to know their strengths and weaknesses and built his own learning curve that would be useful when he became an adult.

Admired by his cohort of young gladiators, he knew that what he had always wanted was attention. It had to be positive or else he would do something that got him negative reactions.

Our mother, when I was in my teenage years, told me some interesting things. The most important thing for me was that William was in fact, not my father. She explained how it had come about and in tears, she sobbed out her story. My real dad was the man who ran the local grocery shop and who employed mum after William was incapable of working anywhere.

The widower, Mr George liked mother and they shared a love life that William was unable to have. Mother told me that our younger sister, Sally, was also a product of Mr George. It explained why Sally and I had blond hair and blue eyes whilst Billy had brown hair and brown eyes.

I was glad when mum, told me that I did not share Billy's father in my genes. It explained why our sibling rivalry was more extreme than with others.

For me, genetics played a huge part in my own protection. Luckily, Mr George was a big and strong man and I had inherited his build. By the time Billy was thirteen, I was bigger and stronger than him and the two-year age gap disappeared. If he hit me, I would hit him back harder and he stopped bullying me and saved his anger to take out on others who could not defend themselves. As much as he enjoyed inflicting physical and emotional pain, he could not take being hurt back.

The thankful thing was that Billy had not turned to drink as his father had and so stopped the need to shout spiteful and cruel words at mother. He had come to appreciate that women are an important part of a man's happiness and spent time getting to know and understand girls at school.

Even after a few years, he still had no idea.

When he was old enough, he got himself a Saturday job at one of Mr George's competitor's shops as mother told him to stay away from where she worked.

He stacked shelves, flattened boxes and wired the cardboard into bundles for the company that took them away to be reused. He stole what he could, not because he wanted the items, but it felt as if he was using resources of others to please himself. He tried his hand at selling in the shop and would smarten up for work.

Phyllis was a regular customer who found Billy attractive even at his young age of fifteen. She liked to use her looks and build to control men. One Saturday, just before closing, she walked, or stumbled in truth, into the shop and told Billy to meet her when he finished. She would be waiting across the road in the phone box. She had been drinking through the day and felt bored and in need of some fun.

Billy checked his hair and tie were straight, washed his hands and walked over to the place he had been told to meet the woman who had told him to do so.

Without wondering why he was following her directions and guided by the streetlights on that mild October evening, he crossed the road and got into the phone booth. He looked around as if she could be hiding in such a small place. He heard a knock on the glass and a finger beckoned him to come out and join her.

Phyllis grabbed his hand and marched away, pulling him as she went as his mother had when he was a toddler. Billy had admired her when she did her bits of shopping before. About twenty, her pretty face, slim figure and bleached blond hair had caught the attention of many men but to be grabbed out of the blue, the young Billy was feeling out of his depth as he had with the girls at school. Men could be handled with a threat or punch, but girls and women were an alien race.

More confusing was, after their arrival in the park and under the cover of the shrubs she, in one movement, put one hand down the front of his trousers while the other hand grabbed his and thrust it up her skirt.

Billy had no idea what to do next. His knowledge of a woman's anatomy had come from watching Sally in the bathroom through the keyhole.

Leaning against a tree, she slid his trousers and pants down, then her panties and guided him into her. After a few seconds it was over and he was confused but happy that he had lost his virginity. Phyllis laughed. 'That was quick. We will need to do it again young man. Hey, I don't even know your name, mine is Phyllis by the way. I liked you because you were always charming in the shop and I needed somebody who would enjoy sex for the sense of pleasure rather than being used by older men who treat females as a commodity for use before throwing them away.'

Billy knew that already. Every time she had come into the

shop, somebody would notice her and say out loud that Phyllis had been looking for something that would make her happy that was not on sale.

The following Monday morning, his English teacher mentioned that he had seen Billy with a woman who looked old enough to be his mother. Billy told him it had been his auntie Bridget who wanted to buy him some fish and chips. The subject was dropped even though the teacher had a puzzled look on his face.

That was the start of a series of training sessions when she would tell him what to do to be a better lover. He learnt fast enough to know most of the tricks he needed to have up his sleeve before Phyllis told him that it would have to end.

Billy did not want that to happen and told her that he was only fifteen and she had had sex with an underage boy. She had even been seen by one of his teachers. On the strength of his coercion, they carried on having occasional routine sex until Billy got bored and ended it. It had to be done that way, on his terms, not hers.

He had learnt more about the use of threat to control and how to use women. They like being charmed and feeling as if they are treasured rather than just objects to give short term pleasure. From now on he knew the lies to tell to get his short-term desires.

His approach to the girls at school changed. 'Hey,' he thought, 'if I can charm the pants off a twenty-year-old stunner, then I can have my way with these girls with no experience.' Including himself, they were all sixteen and it was now legal to have sexual relationships even if the girls were tricked into it by threat and/or by flattery.

Up until the time he left school at eighteen he seduced many girls and raped others who rejected his advances but blackmailed them into silence afterwards.

The amateur now had become the professional abuser.

Forging His Life

Billy knew that education was the key to making money. Through lack of interest in studying, he had failed his 'A' levels and went to work in a bank as an office boy at first and then was promoted to a junior clerk.

He knew that dressing to play the part he wanted rather than the one he had was a key to success. He bought clothes that made him seem to strangers that he was, in fact, the bank manager.

After a few years he joined a big insurance company with his fake degree in business and economics. He was lucky in-so-much as there was no Internet with which to check information.

Billy's degree came easily. While he was working in the bank there was a rumour that one of the customers, a professor at the local university was a homosexual. These were the days when being gay was still a crime.

Billy knew his home address from his bank account details and he would follow him and soon realised that there was one public toilet this man visited fairly frequently. Either he had a weak bladder or there was another purpose. Billy would follow him in and pretend to be having a pee while the professor disappeared into a booth as if he was going to have a shit. Then another man appeared and went into the same booth. Billy then had the method to gain a degree without working for it.

One day he went to the man's house and stated in very simple terms that unless the professor gave Billy a letter on university headed note paper, then his career would be ended.

It needed to say that he was an exemplary pupil and had worked hard to gain his first-class degree in business and economics, the professor's speciality. Once received, he promised that he would destroy the evidence he had against him.

He reminded him that if any company asked for confirmation

of what was in the letter and the Professor gave a negative reply, then Billy would resurrect the information he had against him and make it public. When the vulnerable are threatened then they are too weak to ask for proof. In fact, Billy had none.

I have withheld the name of the university and the professor because I consider them to be victims.

The letter was as follows:

"To whom it may concern, William Mason was a perfect student, very knowledgeable and his ability to learn was exemplary. He was an example to everybody and I wish him well in whatever career he chooses and I am sure that he will make a perfect employee."

Billy started work with no knowledge of the insurance business or how corporations work, but he had a vast encyclopaedia of knowledge about using people for his gain.

He knew that you could control others by threats to their security as well as by physical hurt. Everybody likes to be built up by promises and charm.

His peers at school had either gone off to work or had gone to university. For the next three years his life would be sitting behind a desk doing boring things, talking to people on the phone and honing his skills of control and exploitation to the maximum so when he graduated from the University of Billy, rather than climbing the business career ladder, he would take the express elevator.

One important lesson he learnt from his father was that drink was a friend and enemy, one disguised as the other. He would go for after work drinks with his colleagues of equal status, or even better, seniors and have a nice time.

That would be repeated a few times until the time was right to spike drinks with vodka or whatever else would work to get them drunk enough to make mistakes. The method he liked was ordering doubles for others and singles for himself.

Sometimes they would confide delicate business or personal information that Billy stored in his mind ready to use at the proper time for his own benefit.

He decided that working for a company should really be working for himself. He needed to gain what he wanted and that was a mix of money, sex and acclaim.

He had the ability to dream big. He knew where he wanted to go on the career ladder and spent his first income on buying clothes that made him look like the boss. If he dressed like a winner then that is what he would become. His promotions came fast and he had a team of people who would be able to help him to keep on moving upwards.

Being like a chameleon and being able to change his outward character at will, he used an acronym that was ABC, DEF.

If people were senior to him, 'if Above then Be Charming'. If they were junior then 'if Down then Establish Fear'.

Simple, but he thought it was effective in reaching his goals. He knew that people in work worry about their job security and he could use that as a weapon.

Looking back, his style was similar to the Gunnery Sergeant Hartman in Full Metal Jacket before the film was made. He used put-downs and insults to create fear but he was more subtle because he was in a business that was different to the army. He believed in gain through pain, but the hurt was always felt by others.

He chose his employees, but having an inbuilt distrust of them, once they had served their purpose or had lost his confidence in being able to help satisfy his needs, he removed them in the same way that a gardener dead-headed roses once their attraction had faded and were no longer able to please.

Always a narcissist, he loved himself and his abilities to succeed in all things. He, in his mind, was the best and most certainly better than those who ranked above him at the time. He spent hours in front of the mirror grooming himself and worked his charm to make sure he appeared in every PR photo that bragged about achievement. At one point he grew a moustache and trimmed it to look smart. After a while he thought of his father with his smoke and beer-stained facial hair and shaved it off.

He had a simple strategy. Reduce costs to boost the profit ratios and the easiest way to do that was to reduce staff expenditure on wages. He removed any handsome men who he felt threatened his standing with the women. Women were great because they were cheaper than men and could give equal, if not better, results. Besides, they were more interesting to socialise with and to use if they were willing to give him what he wanted for their security and more money, he thought.

As a reminder of his use of charm and promises, he kept Venus Fly Trap plants in his office, his joke for himself. They would not last long unless the windows were opened, to let flies in so in time they were given to his juniors to look after. He would demand that windows were opened on warm days without giving the real reason. If the plants died then he would berate them in public about the idea that if they could not look after flowers, how could they nurture the customers.

He knew that carnivorous plants attracted what they needed by offering sweet nectar and when the triggers were touched, the flying insects were held by the closing flaps to enable them to be digested. 'What a great way to get what you want. Attract, trap and consume.'

For Billy, charm, flattery and empty promises were his nectar used in his manipulative armoury. Of course, the corpses had to be disposed of with good severance pay and references once used to build his ego and fulfil his sexual needs. He was an expert in putting the offensive into 'charm offensive'.

The women he used were chosen for the one objective. To satisfy him. They needed to be able to work efficiently but he would look at their CVs and application forms to spot his targets.

He would note their pastimes and hobbies and file it away for later use. They had to be attractive and if everything fitted together, they would be employed.

He worked on his plans to grow the business and thereby his rewards.

He would bully people into buying insurance, death plans, by making people feel guilty for not having them. His first line would be 'when my grandfather died the family could not afford a proper funeral and everybody hated him and his memory because he had been selfish enough not to pay for his own funeral'.

By buying into a life insurance plan it meant the people would love the victim during their life as well as after their death. It was his technique for pushing people into paying out money that they didn't have as a guarantee that they would continue to be loved.

He had other plans. He checked out people with potentially high pay-outs on death. He then looked for those who had aged next of kin and who were in a position to receive money with no plans for leaving it to anybody other than charities. He found a suitable target, Mr and Mrs Hardy. He met up with the couple and advised them to invest their money in housing that would bring in rental income which would then be given to their chosen charities. He would be the man to arrange that and 'for tax purposes' the money should go to him as the trustee. They could also sign over their house to ensure that the money was well spent. He needed to wait until the death of one of the couples before he got his hands on their funds, but it would become worthwhile after just a few years.

What Billy wanted was ownership. Not happy to share, he wanted to take over the company and thereby stop any attempts to get rid of him. He knew that the world was against him and worried that even being the CEO would subject him to the scrutiny of a board of directors and shareholders. However, he knew the company was too big for him to own it lock stock and barrel.

A year after his deal with Mr and Mrs Hardy, they died suddenly with just a month between their passing. Billy read about what had happened, rubbed his hands together and spoke to the solicitor about getting the house. When he was told that they had changed their wills and that all the money from the sale of the house and their savings had been donated to a charity for the welfare of donkeys, he became so angry that he threw his phone against a wall where it smashed into small pieces.

He needed a different plan to make money. He decided to bounce the share price by making allies of financial journalists while keeping his identity secret.

He used the information that had been leaked from drunken mouths and would give negative information to lower the value of the company and then buy shares.

After a while he would leak positive information and sell them at a good profit. He knew what he was doing was illegal but he covered his tracks well.

He made enough money during the few years that he managed to get away with it and invested his money in a property which he rented out. He had enough left over to pay for the deposit on a grand apartment that would give him privacy being on the seventh floor where no passers-by could look in.

Relationships

He would rent his house to single women and then he offered an armistice against the rise of rentals by offering his special deal of payment with cash or flesh. He wanted to own the inhabitants as well as the house. After a while, when he got bored with the occupants, he would evict them and select a new woman.

He discovered that lonely, vulnerable and unattached women were the lucrative resource he was looking for. He would get into their minds with a light touch on the arm and then the neck, always moving away to prove that he was after nothing from them. It was a better ice breaker than a few gin and tonics. It worked faster and cost him nothing. If they enjoyed the attention then they needed to move towards him to get more.

He read numerous books on body language and used his knowledge for gain from his work and from the women he wanted. He knew that mirroring another person's position and look endeared them to him. It was another language for being soul mates and pulled them in.

And in conversations, he always liked what they liked. If they liked dogs, he loved them but if they did not like canines, then he hated them. And so he would be like his targets in everything they did, liked or worried about.

Part one was to get them to like and admire him before he put them to the test by being nasty and threatening them that if they did not do what he wanted, then he would break the relationship off.

Of course, what he really wanted was obedience and the expression of their need for him so his narcissistic ego would grow and grow.

He was a perfectionist in many ways, but of course, a narcissist assumes that he is perfect anyway. The victims, the soul mates, had a duty to perceive him as he wanted to be seen or they would be removed from his life.

He needed to be liked for his swagger and charm, all of which had to be shone back at him or they would pay the price.

Fairly, rather really, was a technique he had picked up consciously or subconsciously, from his father. William had blamed his wife for his failings. He preferred drink to food and although mother was a good cook, and used fresh ingredients from the grocery shop, her husband decided that she was a bad chef. Likewise, he accused her of having affairs even though he told her she was too unattractive to find another man. Her lack of beauty was the reason he did not have sex rather than his impotence, he told her.

For Billy, women were fairly good looking because he would never choose an ugly partner so that they doubted their desirability for other men. They were sort of alright in bed but never that sexy. And so it went on. If, in their parallel universes, both were perfect then it did not match his needs. He had to be the best and had to be told as much by the less than perfect woman he was with.

A real relationship is a connexion between two people for the benefit of both. For Billy a liaison was nothing more than an opportunity for using somebody else for his own pleasure. To satisfy his narcissistic needs, he stood on the emotions of others. He would lead them into his idea of a relationship with promises by connecting to their needs.

It was as if he seduced a person to share a ride on a tandem and after a while, he would stop pedalling and enjoy the trip on the rear seat while the suffering front seat occupant did all the work.

For him it was a selling operation by finding the needs of people and fulfilling them and, if they did not know their own wants, then he would invent them for them.

He crept in to lives like a cancer. He was unseen as a destroyer and his targets felt no harm in the beginning but it then took over their lives and the only cure was to cut out the cause, but few knew that.

He made people feel guilty if they seemed to reject him. He wanted them to feel that they had made a mistake if they pushed him away by feeling that they were, in fact, pushing themselves away, not him. The flies that avoided the nectar of the Venus Fly Trap were denying themselves the sweet rewards that were available. If they did not fall for him or showed signs of withdrawal then he threatened that they would be emotionally or even physically hurt.

His technique was straightforward but twisted and devious. To mix metaphors, he was a fisherman. He would bait his hooks and cast them into the water. He needed his victims to swim towards the bait, be pleased with what they found and then start to nibble. Then he would pull gently on the line to pull away a bit and the fish would chase the bait in case they lost it. Then he would wait until the lure was swallowed before pulling on the line to hook the target who could then not escape. When he landed the fish, he would unhook them and return them to the water if they did not fully fit his goals but he kept the unlucky ones.

His techniques were tried and tested. Drinks shared were as before with colleagues. Doubles for them and singles for himself and the need to match drinking rates. No date-rape drugs, just alcohol and his false charm.

He wanted his fish to give him respect, sympathy and to be vulnerable so they felt only Billy could sustain their lives. With the women he caught, he would build a sense of similarity. He would like what they liked after he found out more and more about them.

The objective was to create the sense that the women had found their dream lover, their soul mate who would be there for ever with a real love that they had never found before. They would help him to resolve his problems caused by others. He was a love-bomber and became a coercive controller when he needed to be the centre of everything. Everything he offered was conditional. 'If you really loved me, then…'

Like the fish, sometimes after he had unhooked them his plot would be discovered and the fish would swim away. He was convinced that he had gained when that happened. They had failed to see what a charming and wonderful person he was. Their loss, never his. 'Plenty more fish in the sea.' He would joke to himself as he planned his next angling trip.

Narcissists fall in love with themselves and look for others who will love them in the same way but they never can quite do that as well as him. When they do not seem to follow the rules then the threats start that they will lose the greatest love that had ever presented itself to them.

He would walk away and wait for the calls asking for his love again. The hook had become harder to disgorge. He would repeat what he had done to build that initial sense of love and reliance his victims had for him.

Part of what he did to diminish self-esteem was to remove support and love from others. Friends had to be pushed away and rejected. Family was dealt with in the same way after he had met them and shown what a great find their daughter, sister or niece had made. How could she be so silly as to reject him?

The process was the same as getting somebody addicted to drugs. The victim relied on them for what they saw as happiness and what was needed to survive in the hard and friendless world that they now lived in. Only Billy could save them. He was the supplier in return for them declaring love for Billy and putting up with his abuse.

He, of course was also a victim but he used this to his advantage. Previous partners and girlfriends made his life difficult with their mistrust. They always thought he was having affairs with other women, which he was but never admitted so. His mistrust grew from his deviousness and manipulation of the truth and he would accuse his girlfriends of having affairs when they were not. There was a double bluff. He had suffered because he had been falsely mistrusted and therefore needed the new women in his life to trust him to make him better.

The noose tightened bit by bit so that there would be a compulsion to please him in case he left for good.

The Venus Fly Trap was now closed and escape impossible. The hook was swallowed and embedded in the throat.

He had won. Then he became bored and his need to build his sense of beauty and self worth by finding new prey emerged. He was both a predator and a torturer. Once he had tempted his ladies into his spider's web of deception and illusion, he would push them into a hollow life without friends and relatives who would have helped them to escape before being totally consumed. He made threats that inhibited their getaway and tortured them with emotional hurt. Yet, now and again, his casualties would find freedom with the help of friends who, despite being ostracised, were still there because they saw what was happening. It would take time for the strands of silk to be loosened and the innocent captive could recognise her situation and act to find freedom from the emotional tyrant.

It never bothered him. It would be the time to move on. He wanted comfort and so he would research his potential targets. It was perfect if they were divorced and lived in a house without a mortgage. He would look at house values on the internet and he was as precise in his planning as an assassin in getting results without being caught out.

Part of his weakness that he never saw in himself was that in work, or with women, he expected loyalty although he was never loyal to anybody or anything. They were his toys that, like in his earlier life, he would destroy if he was unable to possess and own.

He felt that he was the Queen bee, or king in his mind. The drones would build the nest. He wanted to benefit from the steadfast work of others who were sacrificing their lives for the fulfilment of his joy.

A narcissist looks in the mirror lots and lots. He sees himself but in reverse, so he likes to take selfies to see himself the right way round. His problem is that he never sees himself as he really is. He is a person lost in a hall of mirrors. Some make him look short, others tall. Then fat, thin, distorted and so on. He is lost because he spends so much of his life looking for the one mirror that shows him as he knows he is; the perfect man. That makes him dependent upon the opinions of others who he trains to give the right answers for him.

He wanted the devotion that cult leaders had and based his relationships on hope and fear. His victims hoped he would change and improve their lives and their fear came from the feeling that he would not be as devoted to them as they were to him. Yet that was the impossible dream. He was only committed to himself.

They hoped that they could help him to become the original charmer that he was when they had met and the fear was that he would leave them if they could not.

The Escapees

There were potential victims of his controlling and abusive ways who escaped the spider's web; the jaws of the predator of emotions; the lure of deadly nectar in the plants that consumed those they attracted.

It always took time for the truth to show itself through the haze and fog of deception to expose the monster that was neatly disguised as the hero, the saviour, the soul mate.

The time taken would depend upon what was being done. It was always after weeks, months or years before the chrome wore off to expose the ugly rust hidden beneath the shiny surface.

Some friends of the victims who did not accept the sudden rejection of a buddy would find ways to penetrate the defences and talk to the casualties. Often pushed away because the friend was assumed to be jealous of such a perfect relationship, the trap was reinforced despite the inner emotional mind having doubts.

When self-belief is lost then there are only the beliefs of the narcissist to guide behaviour. The fly still consumes the nectar of the trap up until it starts to be eaten alive. Escape was not always an option but the women who broke out were not flies, they were people who could research, talk to others and build enough strength to stop their lives from being taken away by a parasite.

And that is what Billy was, a blood sucker who lived on his ill gotten gains from businesses, the innocent people who believed his insurance pitches as well as the women whose lives he stained, hopefully just in the short term before they rescued themselves or who were salvaged.

There was a price to pay, however. After a hunter attacks there are scars. Maybe bruises and marks. Perhaps financial problems. There are always emotional wounds, however, in every case that need to be healed, not with ointments or splints but by talking to trusted friends who will reassure the victim that they were not foolish, stupid, idiotic or weak minded but they were trapped by an expert in the manipulation of innocent people.

I wrote this from the bits and pieces I recalled from his bragging as a young man before he left home and disappeared from my life. I spoke to some of his victims who I contacted after I took his keys for his grand apartment and by using his address book and phone while he was dying in the hospice. They were happy to tell me what he was like and what he did. After I told them that Billy was dying, they often spoke to me as if in a confessional as a way of cleaning the vile remnants of their user.

Others I had tried to contact had blocked any contact from him as a means of escape and so they were unaware of what was happening to the man who had polluted their lives.

One person I called, Shirley, filled me in with a lot of detail. She was reluctant to talk to me at first as the brother of the man who had damaged her but she returned my call after a few days and talked to me as if she was on the couch of a therapist.

I never met her but she had obviously been locked in a mental cell but with the news of Billy's coming demise, she opened up.

I will share her story in my words from what I remember of what she said.

I wish I had recorded her outpouring but that would have put pressure onto a victim who had been pressured enough into her submission.

His lies jumped out as he had tried to build his need for her to be sympathetic. One was about how the scar on his arm came from defending a girl who was being threatened by a man with a knife in a night club. He had fought him off even though he had been stabbed. The truth was, and I knew it, he had fallen off his bike while trying to do a wheelie and had cut himself on the handlebars.

Like most things in his life, he did his best to take advantage of others by inventing a new truth about himself.

Back to fishing. He threw ground bait into the water and then sat back until he was approached. He did this on dating apps, grooming his prey with sweet words, compliments, mirroring them until he was able to reel them in. This was how he had caught Shirley who had fallen for his lines, literally, and she was left craving the attention of the man who was, in her mind, her soul mate.

Her story was much longer than I have written down but I needed to avoid giving away too much detail of the methods he used to protect readers from the huntsmen who might want to use this as a training manual.

She described Billy as an emotional parasite who slowly took over by sucking her life out but leaving enough for the host to live on, albeit weakened and drained.

However, she eventually took control of her own life for herself when a hand written note was delivered to her house while Billy was away. It told her that her aunt had died and gave the details of the funeral. There was also a piece that said Julie, her cousin was worried that they had lost contact and that she neither answered her phone nor replied to social media messages because she had been blocked.

Shirley had loved her aunt and felt guilty that she had not known about her passing. She took a deep breath and decided she would go to the funeral. When she told Billy he became extremely angry and accused her of arranging a meeting with a lover.

She showed him the note and told him when, where and with whom she would meet. He reluctantly agreed but while she was travelling, when she was at the funeral he messaged her continuously. Her cousin asked who this was who was constantly checking on her and Shirley avoided saying. She said that she was not going to the wake because she needed to get home. Then Julie took her to the side outside the church and told her about her ex-boyfriend who was a control freak. She had recognised the signs and, as if in simple conversation and with no questioning of Shirley, Julie said that with her lover, the constant calls when they were apart were to check on where she was and what she was doing and the need to confirm that she was not meeting up with other men.

The tale of woe she told fitted what had gone on with how Billy was, perfectly. Shirley burst into tears and explained what was happening to her. The threats, the accusations, the control and her fear of having contact with anybody other than Billy. She asked Julie how she had got away and realised that the very people who could help her were the ones who he had made her banish. All the time, her phone pinged and after a while she stopped reading his messages and blocked him.

They both attended the wake and Julie followed her home in her car. When they both arrived at the door, Billy came storming out with his fists in the air. Shirley told him to pack his things and go. He at first refused, told her how much she would miss him and then went into a torrent of abuse. He even accused her of having a lesbian lover when he saw her cousin.

Julie stepped in, told Billy that she had videoed what was going on and told him that she would call the police if he did not go immediately. He swore at her and moved towards her aggressively just as her strong looking brother and his friend pulled up, got out of the car and told him to do what he had been instructed to do or they would 'hurt' him. That order was given in a very hostile way that gave Billy no choice. They waited until he had packed, loaded his car and got in to the driver's seat and had driven away.

The message that they would come back and sort him out if he tried to return was not spoken, but implied.

Billy went off to search for his next victim and Shirley never heard from him again. He had been blocked from her phone and from her life.

Real friends offer genuine love expecting nothing in return. False friends, the narcissists, the coercive controllers only offer hurt in exchange for their desperate need to be praised for nothing.

It took time before Shirley started to resume the life she had before Billy crept into her world and she spoke to her friends to explain what had happened. They were all sympathetic and understood. Some of them had heard about people like him before and offered more support for her.

The Tomb

So I, the half-brother of a horrible man, am the author of this short exposé of that monster.

I am a normal man, happily married, blessed with grandchildren and a polar opposite of the man I went to see burnt in the crematorium. Luckily, Billy never had children who might have been moulded into the same vile shape as their father, but they would have presented competition for the love of the unfortunate mother who was made pregnant by a devil and that would have destroyed her.

I received a phone call telling that Billy was dying and was in a hospice. After many years of no contact, I visited him and found that I had no sympathy. As I said earlier, I took his keys from the drawer next to his bed and told him I would return with fresh clothes despite him never needing anything to wear apart from the gown he lived, and would have died, in.

In his home I discovered too many things that told his life in detail. The photographs of naked women in sexual poses, a large number of mobile phones but hidden away in a cupboard, I found his diary that showed so much, a lot of which I have put in this journal.

I was the only person at his cremation apart from the officials. Mother had died many years ago and Sally refused to even acknowledge that Billy was her brother, especially after he had refused to go to our mother's funeral because he was too busy.

I was there because I needed to see my brother's body destroyed in the hope that the dark memories of his victims would evaporate away in the smoke.

My eulogy was to tell anybody about Billy the bully. Then I hoped that there is an afterlife and he would hear what a horrible man he had been before entering hell.

The people he had hurt would not be there, but the memories of what had happened to his innocent prey would.

In the end everything I heard and remembered were like pieces of a jigsaw puzzle which I had to put together. The picture they made when completed was grotesque and scary. There again, Billy was as shallow as a piece of cardboard in the end, fit only to take apart, put in a bag and throw away which in a way, happened.

I am his brother and, even as he was dying, he liked to boast about how great he was how and he had achieved his goals and being without conscience about the people he had hurt. Yet those goals were hollow and as meaningful as the results from a soccer match the year before.

All those people in his life who were too nice to be glad he was dead can now be relieved that the scars they carried can now be healed.

We hear it said that so-and-so died peacefully and for Billy, unlike his victims, there was no physical pain. He suffered from the hallucinations and nightmares brought about by his mixture of painkillers and my hope was that the experiences of fear would be matched with how he made other people feel.

There was one, told to me by a nurse, where he watched young African women being filmed for a documentary. They walked into the desert and blood red plant spikes suddenly grew out of the sand, attached themselves to the first girl and dragged her down into a hole. The other women pulled her out and burnt her body. Then they scraped flakes off her skull that turned into little crab like creatures before running away and submerging themselves into the desert waiting for the next victim, their source of food. The camera man making the documentary just watched and filmed with no attempt to rescue the poor girl.

He had told the nurse the story of his nightmare with the fear still in his mind.

When I heard it, I laughed. He was the monster who consumed women and discarded the remains. Perhaps something in his mind, in his last hours, acknowledged what he had done to others.

After I laughed, the nurse lectured me on my lack of love and what a wonderful person Billy was. He had even used his last breaths to love bomb her. A dying viper's poison never diminishes even when it has no practical use for it. I choked on her words, laughed again and walked away for the last time.

Specifics about what was to be done with his body were never discussed in great detail, but I was determined to keep my word but, in my way rather than his.

From that failed attempt to find nice things to say about him, I decided to outline his life in far more words under the working title of, 'From the Womb to the Tomb, the Horrible Life of a Nasty Controlling, Abusive, Narcissistic Power Freak.' That might change.

If you were one of his many victims, rejoice in his passing and the relief you will get from knowing he has gone for ever.

I will, I know.

He wanted attention even after he had died. I did my best to keep my promise that he would be interred in a tomb in a large plot after being taken away by a big hearse. My pledge was very tongue in cheek, however.

I wrote on his container the words from 'trash to ash, ash to trash' in indelible ink from a marker pen. I dropped it into a plastic sack and then into the dustbin.

He would have been taken away and dumped where people would not know where he was, but there again nobody needed to know because nobody would mourn him anyway. So his tomb was a plastic pot in a large plot under other rubbish in landfill having been delivered in a garbage truck as his hearse.

In a way that makes me as bad as he was but, there again, the revenge I sought was for a lot of people as well as for myself, mother and my sister and the hurt inflicted would not have been felt because he was dead after all, but the people he injured were alive at the time he was doing it.

Predators work under the cover of darkness where they stalk and catch their prey without being seen. Disguise and camouflage were important to him. Like a buzzard, he flew high and out of sight and then swooped to catch his victims. There was no remorse for him. It was a game of one winner and lots of losers. He made sure he always won but this time, his life had been taken away from him.

There is a punchline. As next of kin, all of his money came to Sally and me and we decided to launder it in the true sense of the word. We made it clean. It went to charities for abused men and women as well as the homeless. Sally and I both knew he would have hated that.

REVIEWS

These stories have a serious purpose. They have been told from the experiences of victims and hopefully they will help the readers to avoid the traps that are too widely available and which are set by narcissistic predators on dating apps, social media, in the workplace, bars and clubs.

To this end, your review would be helpful to allow readers to see the dangers from a safe viewpoint.

Thank you.